Mary Janice Davidson has written in a variety of genres, including contemporary romance, paranormal romance, erotica, and non-fiction. She lives in Minnesota. Visit her website at www.maryjanicedavidson.net

Undead and Unpopular

MaryJanice Davidson

PIATKUS

Visit the Piatkus website!

Piatkus publishes a wide range of bestselling fiction and non-fiction, including books on health, mind body & spirit, sex, self-help, cookery, biography and the paranormal.

If you want to:
- read descriptions of our popular titles
- buy our books over the internet
- take advantage of our special offers
- enter our monthly competition
- learn more about your favourite Piatkus authors

VISIT OUR WEBSITE AT: www.piatkus.co.uk

Copyright © 2006 by MaryJanice Davidson Alongi

First Published in Great Britain in 2006 by
Piatkus Books Ltd.,
5 Windmill Street, London W1T 2JA
email: info@piatkus.co.uk

This edition published 2007

First Published in the United States in 2006 by
The Berkley Publishing Group,
a Division of the Penguin Group (USA) Inc.

The moral right of the author has been asserted

*A catalogue record for this book is available from
the British Library*

ISBN 978 0 7499 3799 7

Typeset in Times by Palimpsest Book Production Limited,
Grangemouth, Stirlingshire

Printed and bound in Great Britain by
Clays ltd, St Ives plc

For Mr. Fogarty,
who got me my first rejection slip.

ACKNOWLEDGMENTS

No one comes up with a book totally on their own—if that was the case, authors would get 100 percent of the royalties. Some of the people who helped themselves to my cut, or should otherwise start charging me for their services:

My editor, Cindy Hwang; the entire Berkley Sensation team; my agent, Ethan Ellenberg; Darla (from Team Laurell K. Hamilton); my PR guru, Jessica; my husband Anthony; my sister Yvonne; and the rest of the good-looking bums who comprise my family.

Special thanks to my grandpa for inspiration. If he can escape from a nursing home, I can make my deadlines.

AUTHOR'S NOTE

Betsy's thoughts about Antonia and Garrett's new relationship make reference to the novella "A Fiend in Need," an April 2006 anthology release from Berkley titled Dead and Loving It. This book takes place about two months after the events of that novella.

Also, zombies do not actually exist. Um, right? Please, God.

"And the Queene shall noe the dead, and keep the dead."

—THE BOOK OF THE DEAD

"Keep your friends close, but keep your enemies closer."

—SUN TZU, *The Art of War*

"Victory is mine!"

—STEWIE GRIFFEN, *Family Guy*

Undead and Unpopular

CHAPTER 1

"There's a zombie in the attic," George the Fiend informed me over breakfast. His voice was a calm pond, and he wiped blond strands out of his face carefully as he peered at his knitting.

"Sure there is," I replied. My casual response was, I decided much later, a massive mistake. I mean, here was this guy (vampire) living in the house owned by my best friend with at least three other people (two more vampires and a surgical resident), telling me what the problem was (a zombie), in plenty of time to do something about it, and I totally blew him off. Were this a horror movie and I, Betsy Taylor, Queen of the Vampires, was on the screen pulling this crap, everybody in the audience would have thrown their popcorn and Sno-Caps at the screen.

But this wasn't a movie, so I screwed up in an honest sort of way.

Also, I was distracted, crow-like, by the big shiny thing on my finger: my engagement ring. Pretty silly for someone who was supposedly already married (to the prophesied Vampire

King for the next thousand years) and officially engaged (to same, one Eric Sinclair) for several weeks. But, my God, getting Sinclair to cough up a proposal had been hard enough. I was still stunned he'd come up with a ring, too.

In fact, I was still tingling from our whole previous evening together, a wacky outing involving blood-drinking, sex, a stop by Caribou Coffee for hot chocolate, and The Ring: a delightfully shiny gold band strewn with diamonds and rubies.

I'd had to make a Herculean effort not to squeal when he slid it onto my finger (where it promptly slid off; I have freakishly small hands). Now here it was, a day later, and I couldn't stop staring at the thing.

Also, it wasn't really breakfast, since neither George nor I were eating and it was eleven o'clock at night. But we still called it breakfast, since that's when Marc (the surgical resident) would often get up and have a muffin before his overnight shift.

George—well, actually, we learned his name was Garrett shortly after he began speaking—went back to the lovely baby blue afghan he was knitting, which matched the fine sweater I wore that evening. I, in turn, went back to the guest list. Not for my wedding. For my surprise birthday party. Which wasn't a surprise at all, but I wasn't telling.

It was a short list. My mom; my dad; my (sigh) stepmother Antonia; her BabyJon; my landlord Jessica; my fiancé Eric Sinclair; Marc; my sister, Laura; Garrett's mate, the other Antonia; our friendly neighborhood police officer Nick; Sinclair's friend Tina; former vampire hunter Jon; and of course Garrett. Almost all of these people I had met *after* I died.

Of course, half of these guests *were* dead people. Even Marc, who was alive, often put it, "Why not be dead? Most of my ex-boyfriends act like I am anyway."

Jessica and I kept trying to fix him up, but the few gay guys we knew were not Marc's type. Not that we had any idea what Marc's type was. On top of that, fixing people up is hard. Almost as hard as—well, trying not to drink blood.

I tapped my pencil on the pad, trying to come up with a plan to tell Eric before the wedding that I had decided to completely give up the blood-drinking thing. I figured being the vampire queen had a few advantages—as it was, every vampire I'd ever known had to drink every day, even Eric. But I could go up to a week without so much as a drop of O-neg, without any shakes or desperate pleas for stray rats. So in honor of my birthday, and of being in this shit queen job for a year, I figured I'd give it up completely. I would be in a blood-free zone!

But Eric would be tricky. Normally he ignored whatever I did, but during our intimate moments, someone always got bitten. Sometimes more than once. It squicked me out to try to explain it, but drinking during sex just made the whole thing better—

"Lame, Betsy," Jessica said, coming into the kitchen and glancing over my shoulder as she headed for the espresso maker. "I can't believe you're making a list of birthday presents. Miss Manners would be rolling in her grave."

"Miss Manners is still alive. Besides, it's not a list of presents. It's a list of people you're going to invite to my surprise party."

Jessica, a painfully skinny nag with gorgeous skin the color of Godiva milk chocolate, laughed at me. "Honey, it hurts me to say this. Like a sliver in the eyeball. But we're not. Planning. A party."

"Although," I added, "you don't have to try too hard to get the Ant there. I wouldn't mind if she missed it."

"Sugar." She gave up the espresso maker as too complicated—this was a nightly ritual—and fixed herself a glass of chocolate milk instead. "You made it perfectly clear two months ago: no party. And we believed you. So stop making guest lists and worrying about your stepmother showing up. It's not happening."

"Are we talking about the nonexistent surprise party?" Tina asked, startling me as her bare feet slid noiselessly across the spotless shamrock green kitchen tile.

"I'm putting bells around your pretty, petite ankles," I told her.

Jessica had nearly choked on her drink, Tina had so startled her. She took a breath and said, "She tells us our lives won't be worth living if we throw her a party, then she makes a guest list."

"Constancy, thy name is Queen Elizabeth," Tina murmured as she slid her tiny butt onto the breakfast nook bar stool next to George—dammit, I mean Garrett. She was dressed like the most tempting college student in creation, as usual—long blonde curls, big pansy eyes, knee-length black skirt, white designer T-shirt, bare legs, black pumps. Most college students nowadays hadn't witnessed the Civil War, but undead bomb-shells like Tina just didn't let go of their perky tits.

"What do you want for your birthday, Majesty?" she was asking me as I stared jealously at those ageless melons. Her duties nowadays were the equivalent to serving as "best man" to Eric, whom she had turned into a vampire decades ago. Nowadays, instead of sucking his blood, she limited herself to smoothing out the morning edition of the *Wall Street*

Journal, fixing his tea the way he liked it, and setting out gobs of paperwork for him to look through. "Some nice shoes, I suppose."

"You suppose wrong," I replied. "I want peace on earth, goodwill toward men."

"Do they have a store for that at the mall?" Jessica asked innocently. "Or maybe one of those sales carts in the walkways, right next to the portrait artist and the guy selling T-shirts with pithy sex jokes?" She was shamelessly stealing peeks at the memos Tina laid out neatly on the marble countertop.

"It'd be the only thing they don't have," I said. "Tina, Jessica, I know you. I know I told you not to throw a party, and that therefore you will throw one. But if you want to keep up the conceit—fine. No party. Instead, find a quiet moment to pray for the aforementioned world peace and global harmony, or failing that, snag me a fat gift card from Bloomingdale's."

"Or perhaps a pair of the new Prada loafers," Jessica added.

"No, I'm sick of loafers. Spring is here—I want some strappy sandals." Which was kind of silly—I couldn't wear them with socks, and these days my extremities were pretty icy. But still. I was sick of winter, and this was Minnesota—we had at least two more months of snow.

"Right," Jess said. "Because you don't have enough of *those*."

"Why don't you take one of my existing pairs and shove them up your cute black butt?" I suggested sweetly.

"Well, Ms. Taylor, why don't you take your delicate ivory nose and—"

Tina interrupted the argument *du jour*. "Majesty, are there any designer shoes you don't like?"

Garrett cleared his throat as he started a different stitch—

knit, garter, crochet—it was all the same to me. "She doesn't care for Rickard Shah sandals. Especially the gold ones."

"This is true," I confirmed. "They're all like something out of the *Boogie Nights* prop drawer. I mean, what year is this? I'd pay two hundred bucks *not* to wear them."

"No need for that," Eric Sinclair said, ignoring my yelp and Jessica's flinch. He was worse than Tina. Where she slithered silently, he teleported like an alien. A tall, broad-shouldered, dark-haired, dark-eyed, yummilicious alien. "You have a thousand pairs of sandals."

"Do not. Leave me alone and read your papers."

"Guest list?" he asked, leaning over my shoulder and peering at my pad. "But you don't want a party."

"You're damned right I don't!" I slapped my notebook shut. In fact, I didn't. I was pretty sure. "How many times do I have to say it?"

Don't get me wrong: I can hear myself. And I'm very self-aware, regarding all my little tics and annoying quirks. Nothing triggers Maslowian self-actualization like getting body-slammed by a Pontiac Aztek.

But no matter how bad I sound to myself, I can't help it. My situation is impossible. You'd be amazed how often I'm ignored, even though I am the so-called Queen of Vampires. Repeating myself ad nauseum was one of the many ways I tried to make myself heard. I was too new to the game to be quietly tough, like Sinclair. Wasn't smart like Tina. Wasn't wealthy, like Jess. Wasn't an all-seeing ghost, like Cathie. Wasn't a clever doc, like Marc; or an indifferent psychic werewolf, like Antonia. You know what it's like to be called a queen and have the least to offer among all the people you know? It's a huge ego hit.

"We got it, Betsy," Jessica was saying. "No party. Fine."

"Fine."

"Why are you—" Sinclair caught Jessica's frantic arm waving. "Never mind. Are you ready for our guests?"

"Guests?" I tried not to freak out. They *were* throwing me a party! Bums! And throwing me off by having it two weeks before my actual birthday.

He sighed, which was about as close as he got to a blitzing tantrum. "Please don't say *'guests?'* like you don't remember the European delegation coming at midnight."

"And Sophie and Liam," Tina added, looking over her own memos.

"I know. I *know*." I did know. Sophie and Liam I didn't mind—Sophie was a charming vampire who lived in a tiny town up north with her very alive, thirty-something boyfriend Liam. They'd been a couple for a few months and a while back, they'd helped us catch a real creep, a vampire who got his rocks off dating college girls, charming them into deep love, then talking them into killing themselves.

Sophie, in fact, had kind of renewed my faith in vampiredom. It seemed to me that most of us were jerks, men and women who found sexual pleasure in felony assault. But Sophie was made of purer stuff—the evil that supposedly consumed the undead didn't seem to touch her.

So her coming tonight, along with the pleasant (if somewhat dry) Liam, was great by me.

But this European delegation was just what I didn't need: a bunch of ancient vampires with stuffy accents dropping in to irritate me two weeks before my birthday. As if turning thirty last year (and dying) hadn't been traumatic enough.

"I didn't forget," I said. Truth. I just had been trying hard to ignore it.

He smoothed his dark hair, which was already perfectly in place. Uh-oh. Something was up. "Um, Jessica, I wonder if you could excuse—"

"Don't even," she warned him. "You're not kicking me out of my own house to have a dead-only meeting. Marc depends on me to pass on full reports of the crazy shit you guys are up to."

Eric said something to Tina in a language I didn't know. Which meant, anything but English. She replied in the same gibberish, and they talked for a minute.

"They are totally debating whether to kick you out or not," I said to Jess.

"Duh."

"Let's speak our own language: we'll call it English, which really fucking rude vampires don't understand."

I glared at the two of them; but Tina and Eric kept babbling. I wasn't sure if they were ignoring me or honestly hadn't heard, so I took the mature route and just spoke louder.

"IT'S PROBABLY A SAFETY ISSUE. YOU KNOW WHAT ASSHATS THOSE OLD VAMPIRES CAN BE. THAT'S WHY THESE TWO GET OFF ON INVITING THEM OVER. ANYWAY, ONE OF THEM WILL PROBABLY TRY TO CHOMP YOU, AND WE'LL HAVE A BIG WICKED FIGHT, ALL OF WHICH WE CAN AVOID IF YOU JUST HANG IN THE BASEMENT WITH GARRETT."

"No, no, no. My house. No offense, Garrett."

Garrett shrugged in response. He hadn't offered much since his Shah sandal observation, and literally stuck to his knitting. He had been spending more time than usual in the kitchen: his girlfriend, a werewolf who never turned into a wolf, was in Massachusetts. Apparently her pack leader's wife had had another baby. She bitched, but she went. Garrett stayed, which was fine by me—it wasn't like we didn't have the room. Antonia could come back with half the pack and we'd have the room.

I had to admit, I had no idea what Antonia (the werewolf, not my stepmother) saw in him.

Sidenote: how weird was it that I knew two women named Antonia? Jessica claimed it all had Some Deeper Meaning, but I figured I was just lucky.

Back to my fretting about Garrett. Don't get me wrong. I mean, he was great-looking (it was the rare vampire who wasn't), but I had the impression he wasn't the sharpest knife in the drawer. Not to mention, a few weeks ago he'd been running around on all fours and drinking blood by the bucket. Antonia was smart and, even if she'd been a drooling idiot, she could see the future. Hello? *See the future*. She could have had anybody, I figured.

She would have disagreed. Violently. It was amazing to me that a great-looking brunette with the body of a swimsuit model who could *see the future* had rotten self-esteem, but there it was. And who was I to judge? Garrett and Antonia had a good thing.

"Very well," the questionable prize I was dating said at last, in English. "You may stay. But Jessica, please watch what you say and do. Don't look them in the eyes for long. Speak only when spoken to. Yes sir, yes ma'am."

"Sit up. Arf," I teased.

"What about her?" Jessica cried, pointing in my general direction. "She's more in need of an etiquette lesson than I am."

"Yeah," I said, "but I'm the Queen. With a capital fucking

Q. Hey, you're looking me in the eyes for too long! Eric, make her stop!"

"Give me a damn break," she muttered, and went upstairs making gagging noises.

CHAPTER 2

The doorbell rang as I watched Jessica rant her way up the foyer stairs. She had seemed especially prickly in the past few weeks. Not that I wasn't used to her speaking her mind; she was my best and oldest friend—we'd shared lipstick in junior high. Which, given our skin hues, was a true testament to our friendship (and more importantly, our ability to find common accessories). But it seemed like everything I said and did was going beyond surface irritation, and digging deep inside her annoy-a-meter.

"It's Sophie and Liam," Tina informed us from the foyer.

"Oh, good," I said, following everybody (except Garrett, who was deep in mid-afghan) out of the kitchen. "The fun meeting first."

"Nonsense," Eric said. "All meetings are fun."

I snorted, but didn't say anything. Truth be told, I was too busy looking at his black-panted butt, which was very fine. He was wearing a dark suit as usual, a perfect complement to his dark hair and eyes. He was so broad through the shoulders

I often wondered how he fit through doorways, and had long, strong legs. I pondered the fact that I'd resisted his evil charms for so long.

Although these days, it felt like he was resisting mine. He'd dodged every wedding meeting we'd had. At least we'd agreed on the date: July 31. Sometimes it seemed like forever, and sometimes it seemed like the date was rushing up on me. And I was virtually planning the entire thing by myself (well, with Jessica's occasional help). He had no opinion on flowers, food, drinks, tuxes, gowns, ceremony, or the wedding song. If I didn't know for sure he loved me, I'd think he didn't—

"Your Majesties," Sophie was saying, bowing to us both. Tina had opened our enormous cherry front doors, and there were Sophie (Dr. Trudeau—she was a vet) and Liam, uh, whatever his last name was.

Sophie was dressed in a sharp navy suit with a cute short skirt, matching turtleneck, black tights, and black (ugh!) running shoes. I know it's practical for career women, but sneakers with suits? Jesus couldn't possibly weep harder than I did. Like all vampires, Sophie was ridiculously beautiful, with black hair (done up in an unfashionable bun) and pale, velvety skin. Her dark eyes didn't miss a flea. Which, in her line of work, was probably really good.

Liam was in jeans, leather jacket, and beat-up loafers. Which reminded me again that I was ready for spring, and sandals. It was always startling to see his youngish face (Late thirties? With the farmer's tan, it was hard to tell) juxtapositioned against his prematurely gray hair.

Tina led us all into a parlor (there were at least four; don't get me started) and the first thing Sophie did when we were all seated was hand me a copy of that day's *Star Tribune*. "Would you please sign your article?" she asked pleasantly in the charming French accent she had never lost, not even after all these years here in Minnesota.

Eric muttered something under his breath that, luckily for him, I didn't catch. I had a weekly "Dear Betsy" column for vampires. It was supposed to be published in an undead-only newsletter, but someone had leaked it to the *Trib*. The editor had thought it was hilarious and published it. Most people who read it thought it was a tongue-in-cheek thing. This was the only thing that spared me from Eric and Tina's wrath.

"I'd be glad to," I said. "Uh . . ." Tina handed me a pen. I never had a pen, a leash, or a stopwatch when I needed one. "Thanks." I scribbled my signature on the latest ("Dear Betsy, my friends keep insisting on having their book club meeting during daylight hours. Should I tell them what my problem is, or lie?") and handed it back.

"Heh," Liam said. "Bet the librarian didn't like that much."

He was talking about Marjorie, who ran the vampire library down in the warehouse district, and the column, which was in a paper anybody could read, anytime. And he was right. She had been furious. She was still trying to track down who'd given my columns to the *Trib* editor. I didn't think it was a deep dark plot or anything; accidents happened. I was alone in this theory. Which was why I kept writing the columns, no matter how irritated everyone got.

"Never mind," Tina said hastily. "How are you both?"

"We're real good," Liam replied in his flat Midwestern drawl. Looking at him, you'd never know he was rich. His dad had invented the first pocket calendars with three-hole punches, or some such thing. "Real good. And you're looking good. The same, in fact."

"Oh, well." I modestly patted my hair. There were a few advantages to being a vampire, and not looking my age was big number one. I'd never need highlights again. "What can I say? How're things up in Embarrass?" What a dorky name for a town.

"The same." Not real chatty, this guy.

"Majesties," Sophie offered. "We have a reason for stopping by, if you don't mind."

"And miss all the scintillating small talk?" Jessica muttered from the back of the room. She had used her brief time upstairs to freshen her jack-o'-lantern lipstick.

"Truth be told," Liam said, ignoring the snarky comment, "it's about me. And my age. Sophie's—well, you know—but I'm not exactly standing still. We were thinking about her turning me. We wanted to know, er, um, well, what you thought about that."

At first I had no idea what he was talking about. "Turning you into what? A Republican?"

"A vampire, dumb shit," Jessica said. I bit my tongue and let that one pass, but made a mental note to get her alone and find out just what had made the incredible upward journey deep into her large intestine.

My jaw went slack with horror as I turned back to the happy couple. "Why would you want to do *that*?"

They looked at each other, then at me. "Not everyone has the same view of the undead as you do, my queen," Sophie said. "And I have lost too many lovers to death."

"Oh," I said, because nobody else was saying anything. "Well, that's a shame. Uh. Liam? You, uh, think this is a good idea, do you? Because loving a vampire and being a vampire—those are two very different things. One can be very nice. The other can be pure hell." Eric moved perceptibly at this comment, but didn't say anything.

"I'm not real keen on giving up salmon hash and fried eggs," Liam replied. "But I'm less keen on giving up Sophie. The idea of eternal love—it's . . . well, it's—"

"He's dying," she explained.

"What?" Jessica and I squawked in unison.

"He's only got thirty, forty years left—assuming he doesn't get run over by a bus or hit by lightning." Or have a heart attack from all the fried eggs. For the first time, her smooth face was anxious. "I don't think we dare wait much longer."

Leave it to a vampire to think a healthy guy in his late thirties or early forties was on his deathbed. "Uh . . . Sophie . . ."

Eric spoke up for the first time. "Dr. Trudeau, you know the risks."

She nodded.

"Right," I said. "The risks. The many, many risks. Let us count the risks. Such as." I coughed, stalling for time. "Well, the risks are . . . very risky."

Jessica rolled her eyes, but Tina kindly jumped in. "Sophie, Liam, as Her Majesty is trying to explain, vampirism is a virus—and some people don't catch it. They just die. And young vampires are feral—they don't know themselves, or anyone. Only the thirst. The Queen here is the exception."

"Which is why she's the boss lady around here," Liam said. "But it's a risk I wanna take. I don't much care for the other choice."

"Dr. Trudeau, you may do as you wish," Eric said, not bothering to consult with me, as usual. "It's not for us to deny you a chance to be with your love."

"Good luck," Tina added.

"Whoa, whoa!" I cried. "That's it? We're not going to talk about it for, I dunno, more than *twenty seconds*? I mean, they did come to consult with *me*, didn't they?" Facing dubious looks from my friends, I turned desperately to the new arrivals. "Liam, come on! We're talking about your potential death by maiming, here! Sophie, think about it—how you'll feel if it doesn't work out."

"Of course, if Her Majesty orders us not to do it, we won't do it," Sophie said stiffly.

"I don't give out orders like that," I said, appalled. What was it about vampires, they couldn't take care of themselves anymore, make their own decisions? "I'm just saying, think it over. Liam doesn't look like he's going to keel over, you know, right this second. What's the rush?"

"I think Betsy's right," Jessica said. Everybody squinted at her, and she continued. "Sorry, I know this is vampire business, and I'm just a mangy human, but from my point of view, it seems like maybe you could think it over a little longer. You've only known each other a few months. Lots of people get married after that long, and then divorce. This seems like an even deeper commitment. What happens if the two of you outgrow each other?"

"No chance of that," Liam said.

"Sophie . . ." I trailed off. I tried to imagine how I'd feel if Eric was human, and I knew I'd outlive him. Possibly by centuries. Could I face him getting old and dying on me? If there was any way to prevent it—"Sophie, it's not for me to tell you yes or no."

"Of course it is," she said, surprised. "You're the queen."

"Right, right. And I really appreciate you coming here . . ." And dumping this ginormous problem in my lap. "But you guys are adults, it's your choice. If you want to go ahead and bite him, it's up to you. I'm just saying—" What *was* I saying? Think it over? Wait for Liam to get older? Who was I to tell them no? I was sort of shocked they'd stopped by to ask my permission about something that was so completely none of my business. "I don't know," I finished, giving up. "Do what you think is best. I'll back you up, whatever you decide. And I believe my fiancé has already agreed with my edict," I added with a sidelong glance at Eric, who held his tongue.

"Thank you, my queen. We will be going forward, I think, but your support means the world to us."

"Yup," Liam said.

"And—"

The sonorous, long door chime rang again.

"Excuse me, Dr. Trudeau." Eric turned to me. "Our other guests have arrived."

Great. More vampire fun and games. Tina got up. "I'll see them in, Your Majesty. Dr. Trudeau. Liam." She excused herself, leaving a nice awkward silence for the rest of us.

"So, uh, when are you going to do it?" I asked. I looked nervously at the plush carpeting, the ornate upholstery, the beautiful tapestries. What if they decided to do it *right here,* right now?

"Soon," Sophie replied.

"Do you want to, uh, stay here while Liam, uh, recovers?"

"Thank you, my queen, but I think we'll be best suited at our home."

"Okay. And you'll, uh, make sure he doesn't hurt anybody when he's, you know, nutty and out of his mind with blood lust?" For the next ten years?

Liam winced (well, he blinked), but Sophie soldiered on.

"My queen, I have experience in these matters. Guarding young vampires—I—all will be as you wish."

Yeah, right. That'd be a fucking first.

"Guess we'd better hit the road, hon," Liam said, standing. Sophie stood. We all stood.

"Thank you for your time, Majesties, and your counsel."

"Are you heading straight back to Embarrass?"

"Tomorrow. Sophie don't like to leave the animals too long."

"Best of luck, Dr. Trudeau." Instead of bowing as he usually did, Eric held out his hand and, surprised, she shook it. "Please keep us posted."

"Thank you, Majesty. We will, Majesty."

"Liam." They shook. They were about the same size, though Liam was a lot narrower through the shoulders.

Liam smiled at us, and the corners of his eyes went all crinkly. I thought of him as a nutty thirsty ignorant young vampire and wanted to cry. But maybe it would work out. Maybe, ten or twenty or a hundred years from now, everything would be fine and they'd be happy together.

And maybe we'd be going north for a funeral in a few days.

"Well, uh, talk to you soon." Maybe. *And if you get out, I'll be staking you soon. But never mind.*

"Yup," he said, typically laid back. *Yup.* Like being chomped and turned was as routine as fixing the wood-chipper out by the cabin.

"Are you sure you don't need anything?" I asked.

"Nope."

Tina came in just in time to prevent my hysterical sobbing. Which was just as well; I had nothing else to contribute. She was trailed by half a dozen stately vampires. I knew from 1's briefing—and by the way they held themselves now—that they were very old, very powerful dead guys (and two gals). The youngest was something like eighty-seven. Which was about as old as Eric.

It was hard to take them all in at once—I saw a bald guy with dark skin, a couple of brunettes, a redhead with freckles (an undead Howdy Doody!)—

"Majesties," Tina began, gesturing to the group that had filed into the room. "May I present our European brethren: Alonzo, Christophe Benoit, David Edourd, Carolina Alonzo—"

Tina did not get the chance to introduce the last two; upon Carolina's introduction, Sophie shot across the parlor and was upon Alonzo in a hot fury of teeth and claws.

CHAPTER 3

I barely had time to get a look at Alonzo—a blade-thin, fine-looking guy with skin the color of good espresso and yellowish eyes, before Sophie was doing her level best to claw his face off. Her speed was devastating. I think only Sinclair could have stopped her but he just watched. All he said was, "The French," with a shrug.

So, as usual, I was the one stuck with the moral high ground. "Stop, stop!" I shrieked. "Sophie, what are you doing? Get off him!"

Meanwhile, Sophie was going for his eyes and a stream of presumably impolite French was pouring from her spittle-ridden mouth. Alonzo did not appear immediately hurt, and appeared able to fend her off. However, she consumed enough of his attention that he did not say a word.

Liam took a step forward—to restrain the love of his life, or help her, no one knew—but Tina wisely knocked him back onto the couch. Jessica scanned the room for something to throw, or, perhaps more sensibly, hide behind. Eric watched,

Tina alongside, and the other vampires observed the skirmish anxiously, chatting to themselves in various European languages. (I think they were European languages. Hell, it could have been Asian, or Antarctican. What am I, a linguist?)

Liam got up off the couch, looked at Sophie and said, "Hon, don't do that," and started forward again. I tried to grab one of them and got an elbow in the cheek for my pains, which would have given me a massive shiner in the old days, and that's when Eric finally said something.

"Enough."

In the movies, everybody would have stopped; Alonzo did, but Sophie was still shrieking and clawing at him, and I saw her tear a huge strip of skin off his shaved scalp.

Eric stepped forward, grabbed her by the right elbow, and tossed her away from Alonzo as easily as I'd have tossed a cardboard box. She caromed off the wall and looked ready to keep rumbling despite herself, but I gamely recovered and stood by Eric's side. I tucked my hands into my armpits so no one could see how they were shaking and piped up loyally, if shakily, "Sophie, he said enough. These are guests in my home."

"Our home," Jessica piped up, glaring at me and ignoring all of Eric's previous advice on the care and handling of ancient European vampires.

"Bastard!" Sophie was as wild-eyed as a rabid cat; I'd never even heard her raise her voice, never mind totally lose it like she'd done.

Alonzo calmly pulled the hanging flap of skin off his head (*blurrrggghhh!*) and said in a pleasant Spanish accent, "The pleasure is mine, señorita."

"You dare, you *dare* speak to me? You dare look at me, be in the same room with me, and not beg my forgiveness?"

"We have met?" I couldn't believe how mild-mannered this guy was. And his very voice suggested a man who could sing, dance, and swordfight all at once—yum. I mean, boo!

A sluggish trickle of blood inched toward his eyes, and one of the vampires behind him handed him a spotless white handkerchief. Of course, anybody else would be slipping on a gigantic puddle of their own blood (head wounds in particular looked so frightening), but not a vampire. And certainly not this vampire. He calmly blotted his head for a moment, watching Sophie with his cat eyes.

"You don't remember, swine, bastard, monster?"

He shrugged with suave innocence.

"August 1, 1892? You were visiting Paris. You went to a tavern. You—"

"Oh," he said carelessly. "The bar girl."

"Don't tell me," I said.

Sophie pointed a trembling finger at Alonzo. "He killed me. He *murdered* me."

"Oh, hell," Jessica said, which exactly echoed my sentiments.

CHAPTER 4

Eric and Tina had steered the Europeans into another parlor; I'd grabbed Sophie and hustled her upstairs. Jessica had followed us. Our last view of Alonzo was an indifferent cock of an eyebrow as he watched her hiss at him on her way out of the room.

"Okay," I said when I finally had her settled in a spare bedroom, and then I realized I had no idea what else to say. "Okay, uh. Sophie. Okay. You okay?"

Sophie dropped to her knees, as startling a thing as had happened in the last twenty minutes, and it was already one for the diary. "Majesty," she said, her fingers digging into my thighs, actually ripping through my jeans, and she didn't notice. "I beg you to kill him—or let me kill him."

I grabbed her wrists and tried to pull her to her feet. Her wavy dark hair had come undone from the bun and was flying everywhere, pouring down her back like a black river. Her eyes stared wildly past my own, into some other space. "Sophie, come on. Please get up. Listen, I can't just—you know. He's—part of a delegation."

I couldn't believe it: I had turned into a politician.

"Oh yes, I see," she said bitterly, staring at the floor. "Diplomatic immunity and all."

"Look, we'll get to the bottom of this. I promise. We'll—"

"There is nothing to get to the bottom of." She climbed slowly to her feet. "He murdered me and you will either punish him or you won't."

"It's just that he's—they're—important. I can't just march down there and, you know, punch him in the brain. Sophie?"

Too late; I was talking to her back. Jessica gave me a wide-eyed look and followed.

We found the correct parlor in short order. Just about everyone was seated comfortably, except Liam. He was standing in a corner and looking at Alonzo with a look that bordered on predatory.

"We are going now," Sophie was saying. If Liam looked like a pissed-off panther, she was looking downright murderous.

"Adios," Alonzo said amiably. If he had had a drink in his hand, I am sure he would have raised it.

"Alonzo," Sinclair said, with a small note of reprimand.

"I will see *you*," Sophie promised, "again."

They left. I glared at Alonzo, who shrugged and smiled politely.

"Tina, perhaps you could get our guests something to drink," I practically snapped. Tina stared at me for a short moment, but then quickly nodded and left the room. Good—she understood I needed to assert authority here. Jessica remained comfortable on a velvet chaise longue, but that didn't bother me—I didn't need the Europeans to see me bossing around a "sheep."

I turned to Alonzo. "This is quite a spot you've put me in."

"Us," Sinclair said.

"Right. Did you do it?"

Alonzo shrugged again. His scalp had grown back. Pretty quick, for a vampire—to get that kind of healing, most of us had to feed first. "I'm sure she's right," he said. "I don't remember everyone I've—"

"Murdered?"

"—bitten, any more than a man of romance can remember all the women he has slept with. But I do not dispute her account."

"Then we have a serious problem. You may have wasted your time making this trip."

"With all respect, Your Majesty, killing people—making vampires—is what vampires *do*."

"*I'm* a vampire," I corrected him sharply, "and I haven't done anything of the kind."

"You are young," one of the women—Carolina, it was—spoke up.

"Don't patronize me, you arrogant Spanish bitch." Sinclair's fingers closed over my upper arm and squeezed; I yanked away. "You have already insulted one of my subj—one of my friends, and you've been here, what? Five minutes?"

"We can leave," another vampire said silkily.

"Great! Don't let the heavy cherry doors hit your blood-sucking asses on the way—"

"Perhaps we can reschedule," Sinclair interrupted. "Given recent events."

I glared at him. "Fuck rescheduling."

"Such American charm," Alonzo began, "but if I might correct Her Majesty on a point of etiquette—"

"Thanks, I'm sure I'd find it fascinating, not; and also, in case you missed the memo, I don't take etiquette tips from murderers."

The dark pools of his eyes narrowed. "I will only take so much insolence, even from a supposed queen."

I rolled up the sleeves of my special, Garrett-knitted, baby blue sweater. "Hey, you wanna go? Let's go. But you won't be picking on a kid waitress this time."

"If Your Majesties wish us to leave," another vampire— Don? David?—"then of course we—"

"What a shame," Tina interrupted politely as she entered the room with a tray of teas and wines. It was as if she had heard the entire conversation—and of course, her ears were good enough that she probably had. She promptly set the tray down on the coffee table and rubbed her hands together. "It seems these drinks will go to waste. But not every diplomatic mission succeeds at first, am I right? This one may take a bit of extra time."

"If you have a spare decade." Jessica smirked from her chaise longue. I couldn't tell if she was happier to see these vampires leave, or to see me fail. Either way, the way she blatantly ignored Eric's advice annoyed me.

"Please come with me, ladies and gentlemen," Tina motioned out of the parlor. "You can get back to your hotel all right? Do you require transportation?"

"Possibly off the tip of my foot?" I asked, dodging as Sinclair reached for me again.

They all stood and bowed. I had never seen sarcastic bows before. Asshats. Then they trailed after Tina like the pack of dogs I was beginning to think they were.

"Not exactly the Yalta Conference of 1945," Sinclair spat. I couldn't decide if he was looking at me with deep sympathy, or fathomless disappointment.

CHAPTER 5

I popped a new piece of strawberry Bubblicious into my mouth and chewed frantically. Like constant tea-gulping and daily manicures, this was one of the many ways I tried to distract myself from the near-constant urge to drink blood.

Come to think of it, tea wasn't a bad idea right now. And Tina's tray was still there, so I got started.

"What are we going to do?" I cried, chomping and gulping and examining my nails. "We can't let him get away with it. Poor Sophie."

Sinclair was rubbing his temples the way he did when he felt a migraine coming on. No doubt, my actions were blameless in this case. "Elizabeth, where to begin. First, Alonzo is under your protection as much as Dr. Trudeau is. Second, he's a member of a very powerful faction—"

"Yeah, yeah, I know. We have to play nice."

"More than that," he said quietly. "We must determine if they are a threat to us. Rather, how large a threat."

"What?"

Sinclair was prowling around the (second) parlor like a leashed tiger. "As you probably do *not* recall—"

"Hey!"

"—they came by to pay their respects, but they took their time. You and I have been in power for a year."

I slumped lower on the couch. "Don't remind—wait. You think they should have stopped by sooner?"

"I know they should have. Taking this long is a borderline insult."

"They wanted to see if you guys could keep the top spot?" Jessica guessed, getting up from her chaise longue long enough to sample some of the wine Tina had brought in.

Sinclair and Tina nodded. Their nods were so hypnotic, I almost nodded myself.

"I believe I convinced them of my staying power when I visited them last summer," Sinclair was droning, "and certainly, I was able to avoid a coup at the time—"

"Thanks again," I said brightly.

"But now they're here. Ostensibly to pay their respects."

"But maybe to see if we've got what it takes," I said.

"Exactly."

"Well." I hated saying anything nice or close to nice about the Euro-asses, but still . . . "They're here now. Right?"

"They're probably still in town, somewhere," Tina muttered. "And I don't know that *borderline* insult is the right phrase, Eric."

"One thing at a time. What are we going to do to Alonzo, on Sophie's behalf?" I asked.

"What do you propose we do to him?" Sinclair replied.

"Huh." That was a stumper. Execute him in cold blood? Spank him? Banish him? Lock him in a room with Sophie and let her finish what she tried to start? "Huh," I said again.

"Can you even *do* anything? I mean, all respect to Sophie, but Alonzo killed her . . . what? Over a hundred years ago? Way before you guys were on the scene. And like they said— it's what vampires do. Not you, Betsy. But you know." Jessica sounded as doubtful as I felt. "Can you punish him for hurting someone decades before you were born?"

"A thorny problem," Sinclair admitted. "I have to admit, one rarely faced. Often, a vampire sired by another either joins forces with that elder, or completely ignores the connection. Many, in fact, do not even remember their sire. Sophie does not fall into any of these three categories."

"Ya think?"

"Darling, no one can understand you with that wad in your mouth."

I had made the huge mistake of trying to blow a bubble, and now it felt like yards of gum were tangled around my teeth. I fingered the chunk at the back of my mouth, glared at Sinclair, and tried to look both authoritative and sympathetic, all at once. "We gotta talk to Sophie again," I mumbled. "And the Europeans, I guess. We can't just leave it like this."

"We will," Sinclair promised, but for once, he looked like he didn't have a clue what to do. As frightening as Sophie's breakdown had been, watching him now actually made me feel worse.

CHAPTER 6

"So I'm meeting Dr. Sophie here to try and talk this whole thing out." I took a sip of my daiquiri. "What. A disaster."

It was the next evening; my sister Laura Goodman and I were having drinks at my nightclub, Scratch. It was finally running the black, which had taken some doing, believe me. Vampire nightclubs were awful—blood-drinking, rapacious murder, disco. I had literally killed to get the clientele to behave.

At least I had a little money left at the end of each month now—I didn't need it, but every girl likes to have a little independent income of her own.

Laura nodded sympathetically. A real bear for sympathy, was Laura. She was a precious-looking lanky blonde with sky blue eyes and a flawless complexion. Long lashes shadowed her eyes and her pretty mouth was turned down in a frown as she considered my problem. She smelled, as she always did, like sugar cookies. She used vanilla extract as perfume. It was an idea I was toying with myself. Not vanilla, but something else out of the pantry. Lemon zest? Paprika?

Laura was my half-sister by my father. Her other parent was the Devil. Yes, I do mean that literally. Long story. She was a sweet-looking cutie-pie with a lethal left hook and a murderous temper. The beast only showed about one time in a hundred; but when it did, enemies died.

"She's coming here tonight?"

"Yeah." I checked my watch. "Any minute. And what the hell am I going to say to her?"

As my eyes wandered around the bar, I noticed all of the vampires in here with us looked tense. Like I cared. I had bigger problems, and if vampires came to the Queen's club because they were too scared *not* to, it was a nice damn change.

Of course, they might be afraid of Laura—she'd killed a number of them a couple of months ago. In this very nightclub—why, right over there. She was quite good at it.

I guess that sounded cold, and I didn't mean to be. I tried to treat vampires like everybody else. I really did. They wouldn't let me. It was just—why did so many of them have to be such unrepentant murderous assholes?

Case in point: Alonzo. He didn't even *remember* killing Sophie at first. Bad enough to be murdered, but to have your killer be so thoughtless and casual about it?

"I'm sure you'll think of something," Laura said, which was nice, if totally unhelpful. "Do you want me to leave?"

"Well, it's just that this is, uh, Sophie's private business. I just wanted to explain why we couldn't hang together tonight, even though we made plans."

"That's all right," she said at once. "I'll go to the evening service instead."

I finished my drink. "Back at church again?" Thank goodness. Her attendance had been off since I first met her, and I was starting to think I was a really shitty influence. Although, as Jessica pointed out, Laura could have a lot worse habits than occasionally skipping the nine o'clock service. Freebasing cocaine was the example she'd used.

Laura looked hurt. "I only missed a few times."

"Right, right. Honey, I'm in no position to judge." I couldn't remember the last time I'd attended church services, although nothing about my vampire-ness prevented me from doing so now. Crosses, holy water, Christmas trees—none of that stuff could hurt me. "I was just. You know. Commenting."

"Well, I'd better go before your friend gets here." She rose, bent, kissed me carelessly on the cheek. "We'll reschedule, yes?"

"You bet. Say hi to your folks for me."

"I will. Say hi to my—to your folks, too."

Oh, sure. My stepmother, who'd given birth to Laura while possessed by the devil and then callously dumped her in a hospital waiting room, and my father, who had no clue Laura existed. I'd get right on that. Then I'd cure cancer and give all my shoes to charity.

I watched her go. I wasn't the only one. Clearing my throat loudly enough to be heard, I glared at the guys scoping my sister's ass until they all went back to their drinks. Sure, the package was nice, but it was the inside that concerned me. Not only was Laura the Devil's daughter, she was prophesied to take over the world. Her way of rebelling against her mother was to be sweet, and *not* take over the world. Which was a good thing.

But we all wondered if—and when—she'd crack under the pressure.

As she marched out, Sophie marched in, ignoring the surly

hostess and zooming in on my table like a Scud missile. She stood over me with her arms crossed and said, "Is he dead yet?"

"I forgot how you take your coffee," I replied, not terribly surprised. I mean, after last night, I'd had an idea how our little meeting would go. "Besides, you could probably use a drink."

She plunked down in the seat next to me. "I fed earlier," she said absently. "Liam insisted."

"I meant like a martini or something."

"In fact," she went on like I hadn't spoken, which was very unlike her—she was usually the soul of French courtesy, "I had to persuade him to let me come here alone. He may have followed me anyway. He—he is most cross. As am I."

"Honey, I was there. I *know* you're pissed. And I feel shitty about it. I really, really do. I'm open to options. What can we do?"

"Hand me his head."

"See, that's just not helpful. You've got to work *with* me, Sophie."

She didn't smile. "With all respect, Majesty, if you are unable—or unwilling—to assist me, then I see no point to this meeting."

"The point is, I'm upset that you're upset and I wanted to talk to you about it. Come on, we'll figure out a compromise."

"Majesty." She speared me with her gaze. "There can be no compromise."

I made listless water circles on the table with my glass. "That's the spirit."

"I am not . . . blind to your position. But you must understand mine. He foully murdered me and must not get away with it."

"Well if you, uh, think about it, if he hadn't killed you, you never would have come to America or met Liam or any of that stuff. Made a new life."

"I had to make a new life," she said as if speaking to a child—a mean, dumb child—"because *he stole* my old one."

"Yup, yup, I hear you."

"I understand your hands may be tied politically." She smiled thinly. "I am, after all, French."

I laughed.

"But understand me: if you cannot act, I will."

"See, uh." I picked up my empty glass, fiddled with it, put it down. "You, uh, can't do that. I mean, I forbid it. Now, I know it—"

I was talking to air. She had gotten up and zoomed to the door so quickly I couldn't track. Vampires sometimes seemed all legs to me—it was like they could take one step and be across the room.

"Hey, you can't do that!" I yelled after her. "I've given you an order! I've decreed! You can't ignore a decree! You'll cause all kinds of trouble! Sophie! I know you can still—what are *you* looking at?"

The vampire at the next table, a skinny blond fellow with a mustache right out of the 1970s, was unabashedly staring. "I like your shoes," he practically stammered.

Mollified, I waved the approaching hostess away. Guy needed a shave, but he had taste. I was wearing my usual spring outfit of tan capris, a white silk T-shirt, and a wool blazer, but I was shod in truly spectacular tan suede Constança Basto sling-backs. Five hundred forty-nine dollars, retail. An early birthday gift from me to me. Sinclair, that sneak—it *had* to be him— kept tucking hundred-dollar bills into the toes of my pumps, and I had quite the Shoe Fund by now.

I crossed my legs and pointed my toe, an old trick that called attention to my (if I do say so myself—there were *some* advantages to being a six-foot-tall dork) good legs. "Thanks," I said.

"I have something for you," Nineteen Seventies said, reaching under the table, and coming back up with—ugh—a muzzled toy poodle. It was wriggling like a worm on a hot sidewalk and making little burbling noises around the muzzle.

"Get that away from me," I almost yelled. I wasn't a dog person. I especially wasn't a fan of dogs that only weighed as much as a well-fed lab rat.

Nineteen Seventies enfolded the curly, trembling creature into his bony arms. "I thought you liked dogs," he said, sounding wounded.

"They like me," I retorted. Another unholy power—dogs followed me everywhere, slobbering and yelping. Cats ignored me. (Cats ignore everybody, even the undead. There's something Egyptian in all of that.) "I *don't* like them. Will you put that thing back in your pocket?"

"Sorry. I thought—I mean, I came here with a boon because—"

"A boon? Like a present? I don't want any presents. Or boon. Consider me boonless. She Without Boon. And if I *did* want a boon—which I don't—I'd rather have some Jimmy Choos."

He nodded to someone else at the bar, a short brunette with disturbingly rosy cheeks, and she rose, came over, got Sir Yaps a Lot, and discreetly vanished into a back room somewhere.

"Jeepers," Nineteen Seventies said. "I guess I messed it up all the way around."

"Messed *what* up?"

"Well . . ." He stroked his mustache, a loathsome habit I had no intention of sticking around long enough to break him of.

"Everybody says that if I'm in town, this is the place I have to come. And that it's best to, you know, spend a lot of money here and all that."

"Oh." Who was "everybody"? The all-vampire newsletter one of the local undead librarians put out? Street gossip? My mother? What? "Well . . ."

This was my chance to say, don't sweat it, my good man. I'm just an ordinary gal, not a dictator-for-life asshole like Nostro was. You don't have to do anything—just try to keep your nose clean. You certainly don't have to come to my bar. But thanks anyway.

"Drink up," is what I *did* say, and sure, I felt a little crummy about it, but hey, everybody's got to make a living.

CHAPTER 7

I groaned when I pulled into my driveway. It wasn't even nine o'clock and the whole evening was crumbling apart. I hated how things had gone with Sophie—and what was I going to do if she disobeyed me? "Disobeyed," ha! Even the word was silly. Everybody said I was the queen, but in my head, I was still Betsy Taylor, shoe fashionista and part-time temp worker. It had been almost a year since the Aztek had creamed me, but it still felt like about two days.

Meanwhile, there was a Ford Escort in my driveway, one that smelled like chocolate—Detective Nick Berry, Jessica's new boyfriend.

Marc's beat-up Stratus was parked next to it. Lucky Marc, he'd missed all the excitement the night before, but it looked like he was on days again for a while.

And a rental car—a Cadillac, no less. The Europeans were back.

It took a long moment for me to open the door of my car. I damn near put the engine in reverse and got the hell out of there.

In the end, I got out and trudged into the mansion. Where was I supposed to go, anyway? This was home.

I zeroed in on the conversation—a third parlor, the one that took up a good chunk of the first floor. I could hear Marc squawking like a surprised goose: "Whaaaaa?"

I hurried down the dimly lit hallway.

"You guys *saw* Dorothy Dandridge?" he was saying as I entered the parlor. He was delighted and surprised, jumping up on the couch cushions like Tom Cruise with a boner. "You saw her live, on stage?"

"Yes, on a visit to New York City." Alonzo was watching Marc like an amused cat. He was sleek and cool in a black suit, black shirt, black socks and shoes. I didn't know the brand—men's shoes all look the same to me. His were spotless and polished to a high gloss, the bows in the laces perfectly tied. "She was wonderful—a joy."

"It was the last time I saw you," Sinclair commented, "before last year." He was more casually dressed—an open-throated shirt, dark slacks. Shoeless and sockless. This was a message, I knew, one for Alonzo: *I'm not worried enough about you to dress up.*

"Correct, Majesty," Tina said courteously. "We left for the West Coast right after."

It occurred to me, not for the first time, that I had very little clue what Sinclair—my fiancé and current consort—had done in the decades before we'd met. One night I'd have to get his whole life story out of him. It wouldn't be easy. When there wasn't a crisis at hand, he was about as chatty as a brick.

"You *saw* her." Marc couldn't get over it. *Boing, boing* on the couch. "Live and everything. Did you get to meet her?"

"Did you bite her?" I asked. I had no idea who Dorothy Dandridge was.

"That's the tragedy of her," Jessica said. She was on the couch beside Marc, trying not to be pitched onto the floor with all his antics. As usual, her hair was up—skinned back so tightly her eyebrows arched—and her mouth was turned down. She was dressed in her usual "I'm not really a millionaire" style: blue jeans, Oxford shirt, bare feet. In the spring! It made me cold just to look at her and Sinclair. Tina, at least, had wool socks on. Marc hadn't even taken off his tennis shoes. "That you've never heard of her."

"I didn't *say* that," I said.

"Oh, please, it was all over your big blank face." Her broad smile was forced—it was clear the barb was genuine, and not at all a joke.

"What is *with* you these—" I began, forgetting all about Alonzo, Sophie, bare feet, only to be interrupted when Detective Nick came back into the room.

"Thanks," he said cheerfully. "I was in the stakeout van half the day—no time to take a—oh." He slowed down. "Hi, Betsy."

I stifled a groan. Nick was a whole new problem, his own subset, you could say. I'd known him before I died. I'd bitten him right after I'd died, and it had driven him nuts. Literally crazy. Sinclair had had to step in with a bit of vampire mojo to make him all right. The official line was: Nick never knew I died, didn't know we were all vampires.

But we all wondered if he was going along with the party line, or fooling us. Normally I'd think nobody could get past Tina's bullshit radar, but Nick was a cop. They paid him to lie.

And Jessica had decided to *date* him. Because, you know, my life wasn't stressful enough.

He held out his hand, and I clamped on it and escorted him to the parlor door. "Great to see you again." I had no intention of introducing him to Alonzo, the Amazing Spanish Killer Vampire. "Guess you two want to get to your date, huh?"

"Actually . . ." Jessica began with a mischievous glint in her eyes.

"Well," Nick said as I hustled him out, "the show starts at ten, so we thought we'd stay and visit for a few . . ."

"Right, don't want to miss it, have some popcorn for me, bye!" I hollered as he practically went sprawling into the hallway. Jessica rolled her eyes at me and followed. "See you later!"

Much later.

"That was," Tina said, stopped, and put a hand over her mouth so I wouldn't see she was fighting a grin.

"Efficient," Alonzo suggested.

"You hush. You're still on my list, chum."

"Oh, Majesty." He clasped his heart like a player in a bad opera. "I would gladly cross seven raging oceans to be on any list you might have."

"Are you trying to pick me up?" I asked irritably, "or overthrow me?"

"Can we not do both, darling Majesty?"

"Say that now," Marc said cheerfully. As usual, he was clueless—or didn't care. He just loved the whole vampire politics thing. It was a lot more interesting than his day job, saving lives.

"Don't you have some patients to intubate downtown?" I asked him pointedly. "Or some dates to fondle uptown?"

"If I did, do you think I'd be here?" Damn. So reasonable, and the truth besides. He looked at Eric and Alonzo again. "So tell me about the show. Where did you see Dorothy? Did she look fabulous? She did, didn't she?"

"I was there for other reasons," Sinclair said. "I must admit I paid little attention to the stage goings-on."

Marc groaned and covered his eyes. His hair was growing out—he'd been shaved bald when I first met him—and his scalp was almost entirely black now, with an interesting white streak above his left eyebrow. His green eyes were shaded with long black lashes—guys always got the good eyelashes—and he was dressed in the scrubs he'd worn to work. They made him look doctor-like and professional, which was good, because he was actually a few years younger than I was, and sometimes patients had a hard time taking him seriously.

They should see him now, bouncing on the couch and grilling an undead Spaniard about somebody named Dorothy.

"As I was saying, it was in New York City," Alonzo said, smiling as Marc sighed and squealed like a bobby-soxer. " 'La Vie en Rose.' Could it have been . . . 1950? Yes, I think so."

"Oh, man, this totally makes my night. It was a shit night to put it mildly. I'm on my third set of scrubs."

"Oh, a lot of patients?"

"Bus crash. A lot of DOTS. Just really a downer."

"DOTS?" Alonzo asked.

"Dead on the Spot," Sinclair and I answered in unison. Thanks to Marc, we were up on all the medical slang.

"That sucks," I continued. "Maybe you should skip work for a while, Marc."

He shrugged. "They're hauling in a shrink for us to talk to, you know, talk about how helpless and arbitrary the whole thing was." He seemed to make a determined effort to look cheerful. "Anyway, you were saying about Dorothy, Mr. Alonzo . . ."

"She was wonderful," the Spaniard said at once, and I almost liked him for his obvious attempts to cheer Marc up. "Illuminating, gorgeous. It was impossible to take your eyes off her. Unless you were the king," he added, with a nod in Sinclair's direction.

"Thanks for not killing her and dumping her in an alley somewhere," I observed sweetly.

"Her neck, her voice box, was a work of art," he said, having the colossal gall to sound wounded. "Risking damage to such delicate organs with my teeth, even for the sake of eternal life, would have been sacrilege."

"And ending Sophie's life was not?"

Marc shook his head sadly, unwilling to completely damn this magnificent Spaniard. "Sophie's a great chick, man. You shouldn't've killed her. A great chick."

"Who would, if my math is correct, be at least fifty years under her cold, stony grave by now had I not turned her. Assuming she died of natural causes."

"That wasn't for you to decide," I said sharply. "Vampires can drink without killing people. You didn't have to take it that far."

He spread his hands. "This argument is pointless. The girl is dead. She hates me for it. There is nothing I can do about this now."

Marc looked at me. "Good point." I could see he was half in love with Alonzo already.

"Go make yourself some Malt-O-Meal," I snapped. "This is vampire business."

"Hey, I know when I'm not wanted." He didn't move from the couch.

"You're not wanted," I said.

"Oh." He got up. "Well. It was nice to meet you. Maybe you can tell Betsy and Sophie you're sorry and, you know, hang out for a while."

"Perhaps." Alonzo held out a hand, and Marc shook it. "A pleasure, Dr. Spangler. I look forward to our next conversation."

Marc was staring raptly into Alonzo's chocolate-colored eyes. "Yeah, that'd be good. I'm off for the next two days, so maybe—"

"Maybe," I said, seizing him by the back of his scrubs, "you shouldn't break your dating drought with this guy."

"Hey, I deserve a social liiiife," he trailed off as I practically threw him into the hallway. It was my night for tossing men out of the room, it appeared.

I stuck a finger in Alonzo's bemused face. "Don't even think about it."

He licked his thick lips. Which probably sounded gross, but it wasn't—it actually called attention to his lush mouth. "I assure you, Majesty, I do not make a move toward that delicacy of a man without your express permission."

"Ha!"

"But it is the truth," he said, sounding vaguely hurt. "Why else am I here, if not to make amends for yesterday?"

"To figure out how to kill me, after a rotten evening?"

He smiled at me. It was a nice smile; lit up his whole face and made him look like a pleasant farmer from Valencia instead of a rotten undead fiend from hell. "Oh, Majesty. Forgive me if I patronize, but how young you are to me.

There was nothing rotten in last evening. Just a simple misunderstanding. To kill you in response—forgive me, to try to kill you in response—would be an overreaction of the worst sort."

Tina and Sinclair looked at each other and I could sense their unspoken agreement: *it's a peace offering. Take it.* As usual, when I was the only one who felt a certain way, I got pissed.

"Look, we can't just paper over this, okay? You weren't here two minutes before you plopped a big steaming pile of shit into my lap. Last night was *bad,* get it?"

"Majesty, lopping off heads and cutting off penises and flaying strips of skin and drying them out like jerky, then making innocent children chew on them, *that* would be bad. Not being allowed to feed until you lose your mind, fighting over victims like dogs in a pen, that is bad. Do you understand this?"

"Alonzo." I ran my fingers through my hair and resisted the urge to kick the couch through the wall. "Okay, I understand. You are trying to put this in perspective. So try to see mine. You hurt my friend. You killed my friend."

"When you were not in power, when I did not know she would be your friend."

"Agreed. But dude: she is gunning for you."

"And you will allow that? Am I not your subject as much as she is?"

"Maybe a caged death match?" Marc hollered from the hallway.

Tina got up and firmly shut the door.

"Perhaps a formal apology?" Sinclair suggested.

"I would do that," Alonzo said at once. "It would be my

honor to do that, to help Her Majesty and His Majesty find a way through this . . . difficult situation."

I sighed and looked at Tina and Sinclair. Of course they would want this to end here, with a hint of a chance at agreement, so we could move on with diplomatic relations.

I gave them both a look. Tina had turned Sinclair; they were best buddies. Of course he would think Sophie and Alonzo could Just Get Along.

"You didn't see her tonight. She is beyond pissed. And she's pissed at *me,* because I'm not helping her. Yet," I added, hoping to wipe the smile off his face. Unfortunately, since I wasn't cutting off his penis or making him eat his own skin, he was in a pretty good mood.

"Where's the rest of the Undead L'il Rascals?" I asked, because more surprises, I so did not need.

"We felt it was better for me to return alone to make amends, as I was the one to, ah, incur your wrath." He almost laughed when he said *wrath.*

"Alonzo, I am fond of Sophie as well," Sinclair commented.

Finally, the lurking smile was banished. Alonzo looked contrite. "I cannot undo the past, Majesties. If you will it, I shall seek out the lady and apologize. And make amends."

"Make amends how?"

"However you wish. My fate," he said simply, "is in your hands."

I glared. "Stop being nice about it."

"Of course, as you wish. I shall endeavor to stop the niceness of my apology immediately."

Before we could go any further down this insane road, there was a long, sonorous *gong* from the foyer, and I nearly groaned. The front door. Terrific.

"You know what? I'll get it. You guys"—I motioned to Tina and Sinclair—"should Alonzo be strung up by his balls? Discuss."

"I would be against that particular course of action," I heard him say as I left the room.

My evil-o-meter must have been on the fritz, because I didn't realize it was my stepmother until I'd swung open the door (these old fashioned mansions didn't have any peepholes—something we probably should have rectified when we moved in).

She was holding my half-brother, BabyJon, a chubby three-month-old infant who was squirming and wailing in her arms.

"You take him," she said by way of greeting. "He's just being impossible tonight, and if I don't get any sleep, I'll be awful tomorrow for the foundation meeting."

"It's not a good—" I began, then juggled the baby as she shoved him into my arms. "Antonia, seriously. This really isn't—"

She was backing down the front steps, wobbling on her high heels. If it hadn't stuck me with permanent baby duty, I would have wished her to fall down. "He'll need to eat in another hour," she said. "But it's not like it's really an imposition, right? You'll be up all night anyway." She'd navigated the steps in her tacky brown pumps, and now she was practically running to her car. "I'll pick him up tomorrow!" she yelled, and dove into her Lexus.

"It's not a good time!" I hollered into the spring night as gravel sputtered and tires squealed. BabyJon was chortling and cooing in my arms. And—was that?—yep. Shitting. He was shitting in my arms, too.

I trudged back to the parlor, laden with bags of baby crap and, of course, the baby.

Alonzo looked mildly surprised. "I thought I smelled an infant," he said, which was creepy in nine ways.

Tina looked away, nibbling her lower lips. Sinclair looked resigned.

"I'm, uh, going to be babysitting tonight. Starting right now. Which does not get you off the hook," I added. "But we'll have to finish this up later."

"You have a baby?" Alonzo asked, looking befuddled.

"It's not *my* baby. It's . . . ugh. You know what? Never mind. Our discussion is over. Go apologize to Sophie, if you think that'll make things right. Just . . . do it and mind your own business."

BabyJon, perhaps in agreement, barfed all over me.

CHAPTER 8

"I had other plans for us tonight," Sinclair said, looking nudely
aggrieved.

I had just plunked BabyJon into the port-a-crib in our room,
none too happy about current events. I was trying not to drool
at my fiancé, who was standing, hands on hips, beside our
bed. His dark hair was mussed from where he'd pulled his
undershirt over his head (vampires layered), which was the
only indication that he was annoyed. With his broad shoulders,
long muscled legs, and big, uh, nipples, he could have been a
lumberjack slumming in the state capital. All he needed was
the axe. And possibly the blue ox.

"This wasn't exactly how I pictured spending the evening,
either."

"Must he sleep in here with us?" Sinclair continued.

"He's not exactly sleeping," I mumbled, as BabyJon cooed
and chortled in the port-a-crib.

"Why not put him down in another room?"

"Why do that when I can put him down here?" I looked at

the baby. "You're fat and you don't know how to use toilet paper."

"I am quite serious, Elizabeth. Put him down somewhere else."

"Eric! Be sensible. What if something happened to him? This is an eighty-room mansion. What if he chokes? I'd never forgive myself if I couldn't get to him in time because I couldn't remember what door I put him behind."

"You have super speed and super hearing." Eric sighed.

"It's just one night. We're supposed to be together for a thousand years, you can't ditch sex for one night?"

"It is the third night," he retorted, "this week. At this rate, in a thousand years we'll have missed sex one hundred fifty-six thousand—"

"Jeez, okay, I get your point, so what? I should put him on the doorstep from now on?"

"You could trying telling your stepmother no."

"It all happened so fast," I said weakly. "And you want him to have to spend *more* time with his mother? Unfeeling bastard! Besides, the baby brings the family, uh, closer together."

"Which I would understand, if you had the slightest desire to be closer to Mrs. Taylor."

"It's one night," I said again. Okay, three—in addition to the surprise she'd dumped on me tonight, we'd actually planned for the baby to stay tomorrow night and Monday. I decided not to bring this up just now. "Come on, babe. He's the only little brother I've got. Maybe he's our heir!"

BabyJon farted.

"Our heir," Sinclair observed, "is a hairless, incontinent monkey. With frog legs."

"That's not true! He looks like a real baby now." About the

incontinence, I couldn't argue. But BabyJon had plumped up beautifully, and wasn't so yellow and scrawny anymore. He had a mohawk of black hair and bright blue eyes. He didn't look like my dad or my stepmother. But who could tell with babies? They usually didn't look like anybody.

"You only like him because he prefers you to all others," Sinclair pointed out.

"Well, sure. Duh. Come on, it's a little flattering that I'm the only one he can stand. I mean, how often does a girl find someone like that?"

"*I* prefer you above all others."

I melted. *Goosh,* right into a little puddle on the carpet. At least, that's what it felt like. "Oh, Eric." I went to him and hugged him. He was stiff in my arms for a moment (not in a good way), then hugged me back.

"You have to admit," I said, nuzzling his chest with my nose, "it's brought us together."

"Us being you and Mrs. Taylor."

"Yeah. I mean, my whole life—since I was a kid—we've basically stayed out of each other's way, when we weren't torturing each other. Now we're almost . . ." I was stumped. "What's the word?"

"Civil."

"That's it."

He was stroking my back with his big hands and I leaned further into him. He dipped his head, kissed me, sucked my lip into his mouth, plunged his fingers into my hair, and I responded eagerly, hungrily, touching him wherever I could reach as we—

"Arrrrggggh," BabyJon said, and an unmistakable, mood-killing odor filled the air.

Sinclair pulled away. "Perhaps he should see a doctor. Certainly there must be specialists for this sort of thing."

"Eric, you're just not used to babies. Stinking up the room is what babies do. And changing them," I said, stepping toward the diaper bag, "is what I do, apparently."

"I'm going to take a shower," he sighed, and trudged into the bathroom.

"Thanks for nothing," I told my brother, who stuck his tongue out.

CHAPTER 9

"Aw," Laura the Devil's Daughter was saying, chucking BabyJon under the chin. "Ooo's a wittle ittle cutie-pie? Is it ooo? Is it?"

"Stop that," Sinclair ordered from his breakfast nook bar stool, "or I will kill you right now."

Laura ignored him. "It *is* ooo! So key-yute!" She shifted him to her left hip and looked at me. "I ran into Mrs. Taylor on the way in. She invited me to a fund-raiser she's chairing."

"She did?" She didn't invite *me*. Not that I would have gone. But still. She wasn't dumping BabyJon on Laura every two days, but who got the invite? Hmmm? That's right, the devil's daughter. "I don't know why she even bothered to stop by. I mean, she had him at her house for, what? Six hours?"

"And now," Tina said, "he's baaaaaack." She snickered at Sinclair, who ignored her.

"Laura, it is quite remarkable." It was the next evening, and he was paging through the *Wall Street Journal*. "You appear to have the capacity to melt the iciest, most unfeeling exteriors."

"You shouldn't be so hard on yourself," I teased.

"I was referring to Mrs. Taylor."

"Did you work things out with Sophie?" Laura hastily interjected. She slung BabyJon over a shoulder and patted him. The smell of burped-up baby formula mingled with the aroma of fresh-squeezed orange juice—Laura's favorite drink.

"Uh, no. No word from Sophie."

"I'm sure it's just a matter of time," she said unhelpfully.

"Right. Actually, it's super tricky because the guy she's so pissed at, he's a big European mucky-muck and super-charming, too. I mean, he's sorry. He says he'll apologize. What am I supposed to be, be all *off with his head*?"

"Technically, you're allowed," Tina pointed out.

"Well, the new boss is *not* the same as the old boss. Which is my whole new, you know. What's the word?"

"Platform," Sinclair said.

"Right. Sympathetic understanding, in. Beheadings, out."

"I'm glad it's your problem and not mine," my sister said cheerfully, because she'd taken Unhelpful Pills this week.

"Actually, Laura, I am glad you stopped by," Sinclair said, glancing at his watch. "We need to have an important, private meeting among the household. I was hoping you could take the infant for an hour or so."

"His name's BabyJon," I said, "not 'the infant.' And what are you talking about? What meeting?"

I heard a car door slam outside and, annoyingly, Tina and Sinclair looked completely unsurprised.

"Of course," Laura was saying. Anybody else so unceremoniously getting the boot would be a little offended, but you had to do a lot worse than that to Laura to irk her. "Glad to help out." She scooped up the diaper bag and left with BabyJon, just as Jessica walked into the kitchen, still in her coat and rubber boots.

"Good evening," Sinclair said.

"Hey," I said, as Jessica dropped her purse on the table and went immediately to the teakettle on the stove.

"Hey," she replied.

"Jessica, we're glad you're here." Tina glanced at me, then continued. "We've been wanting to talk to you. For some time."

We had? Right. We had. I'd been meaning to get her alone and ask why she'd been so bitchy lately. Looked like Tina and Sinclair had noticed, too.

"Super," she replied with a noticeable lack of enthusiasm.

"Dear, is there anything you want to tell us?" Sinclair asked, folding his paper and then folding his hands in front of him.

"Your rent's due?" she suggested, adding a hefty dollop of cream to her tea.

"The check is on your desk. Something else."

"What is this," she joked, "an intervention?"

I didn't know *what* it was. But I could see the white Walgreens prescription bag peeking out of her purse. All of a sudden, I didn't want to be in this meeting.

"In a manner of speaking," Sinclair replied, "yes."

"Jess, you've been a little, uh, touchy lately." I coughed. "Is anything up?"

"No."

"Perhaps," Sinclair said gently, "we can tell you."

She sat. Shrugged out of her coat. Looked at him. For the first time, I noticed the dark circles under her eyes. She hadn't been sleeping well.

What else hadn't I noticed?

"Why don't you?" she replied. "Tell me, I mean."

"As you wish. At first, the change in your scent appeared to be the product of stress. But after consulting with each other, Tina and I quickly recalled the last time we sensed this—condition—in a living human."

"You quickly recalled?" Jessica teased, except she didn't sound much like she was teasing. "Or did you slowly recall?"

He ignored her and continued. "It was shortly after we arrived upon the West Coast, and found temporary shelter in the basement of a nursing home. There was a woman there who suffered for a long time—"

"Can we get to the point?" I hissed, squashing the urge to pull all the hair out of my head. There was no way this story was going to end well.

Jessica shifted on her bar stool and looked at me. I could tell she really, really wanted to say it. But she couldn't.

Sinclair let his hand slide across the marble counter and rest on top of hers. "You have myeloma."

"What?" I said.

Jessica didn't take her eyes off me. "Blood cancer."

"What?" I screamed.

CHAPTER 10

"I knew you'd be like this," Jessica insisted.

"Oh my God. Oh my God!" I was lying on the cool kitchen tiles, a cold cloth on my forehead. "I can't believe this!"

"Darling," Sinclair said, kneeling beside me, "you are my soul and my life, but this is not even remotely about you."

"How can you *say* that?" I cried. "My best friend is *dying—*"

"I'm not dying," Jessica said sharply. Far above me, perched upon her bar stool, she looked more than ever like an impatient Egyptian goddess. "I knew it, I *knew* it. This is how you get. This is why I didn't say anything."

"How could you keep this from me?" I screeched upward. "I told *you* when *I* died."

"I'm not dying," she said again, louder. "I've been to seven different specialists and they're all pretty optimistic."

"Seven? Specialists?" I rolled back and forth on the tile and groaned. "They all knew before I did? I'm like, *eighth* on your to-know list?" Tenth, I realized, when you counted Eric and Tina. "This is horrible! What kind of friend can I be? I've been sitting around chatting with Spanish murderers and you've been hauling your buns to cancer doctors?"

"I wouldn't put it quite like that," she admitted.

"How long have you been sick?"

"I got the diagnosis a month ago." To Sinclair: "Here we go."

"A month ago? Month? As in four weeks, as in thirty days?"

"Thirty-one," Tina pointed out helpfully.

I ignored her. "You didn't think you could *mention* it? You had other things on your mind? Why the *hell* didn't you say anything?" I felt faint, but I was already lying down. That was something. *"How could you do this to me?"*

"I'm sorry." Jessica sniffed. "I guess I was being selfish."

"You're goddamned fucking right you were!"

"Elizabeth."

I turned on them like a rabid hyena. "You guys *knew*? You *knew* and you didn't *say* anything?"

Jessica looked thoughtful. "You two haven't been spying on me or anything, have you?"

"No, of course not," Tina said. She was patting my hand, kneeling on my other side. Jessica slid off the stool and stood at my feet. Tina looked up at Jess and added, "We didn't need spies to figure this one out."

"Also," Jessica said, "that'd be a crummy thing to do to your friend."

"Yes, yes. As Eric suggested, your scent has been a little anemic lately. There are multiple reasons why this might be, but each reason has its own particular, well, sub-scent. When Eric and I put our heads together, we matched yours with the woman in that nursing home. She also suffered from myeloma. It's rare to be that close to someone who has had it for so long, but the sub-scent is distinctive."

"And Betsy's the Queen, and you vampires should always tell your Queen everything. So. One way to look at it is that *you* guys should have told me."

The corner of Jessica's mouth twisted in a wry smile. "That's right, they're the ones who screwed up, not me. It's all on them."

"Nice try," I yelled from the floor. "You are still in a shit-load of trouble, birdbrain. I can't believe this is happening to me!"

"I know," she sighed. "What a terrible week you're having."

I glared up at her. "When I get off this floor I'm kicking the shit out of you. Then you'll *really* need a doctor."

She grinned down at me. "Happy birthday."

CHAPTER 11

The kitchen door swung open before Jessica, Eric, Tina, or I could say another word. "I'm home!" Antonia the werewolf called, Garrett right behind her.

"Not now, Toni."

"How many fucking times I have to tell you? An-TONE-ee-uh. Just because your lousy stepmother has the same name doesn't mean I have to change mine."

"Not *now*."

"Oh." She looked down at me. Garrett did, too. "Jessica finally told you, huh?"

Eleventh!

"Duck and cover," Tina muttered, but I was in no condition to launch myself at our resident psychic werewolf.

"You saw it in a vision?" Jessica asked.

"Hell, no. You smell totally bland. What, you guys didn't know?" Toni was looking around at all of us. With her short, Aeon Flux–like dark hair and big brown eyes, she should have looked more innocent than she sounded. And I didn't know what was up with the old T-shirt and Daisy Duke shorts (and flip-flops! In April!) but right now, her grotesque fashion screwup was the least of my problem. "Huh. Guess I should have said something before I left."

"Think so?" I snarked from the floor. "As your punishment, you are now and forever known as Toni."

"The hell!"

"Jessica's sick," Garrett said helpfully. "Also, there's a zombie in the attic."

"Shut up. Help me up. Goddammit, I'm kicking some serious ass in a minute."

"I'm outta here," Toni said at once, turning to leave. "Just wanted you to know I'm back from the Cape."

"Well *thanks for sharing*." God, she was the most fucking annoying person in the fucking history of fucking people! Ever! Though, to be fair, I may have been feeling overly sensitive at that moment.

"Come on up to the bedroom and welcome me back," Toni was saying to Garrett as they left the kitchen. *Ugh*. I prayed I wouldn't be able to hear them doing it.

"What are your immediate plans?" Sinclair asked Jessica as he grabbed my elbow and lifted me effortlessly to my feet. Apparently, I was done wallowing.

"Chemo, probably. We're still figuring out options."

"How sick are you?" I asked anxiously.

"Not sick at all, compared to how I'll feel when they shoot radiation into me," she said with glum humor. "I'm just tired a lot these days. I actually thought I might be . . . well . . ."

"Pregnant?" Tina suggested quietly.

Jessica nodded. "Yeah. I'd been tired, and I'd—well, there

were other symptoms. And Nick and I—anyway. I was wrong. Definitely not pregnant."

"Does Nick know?"

She looked away. "Nobody knows except you guys."

"Oh." I knew Jess very well, better than anybody (I was pretty sure), and I knew why she hadn't said anything. I didn't like it, but I could figure it out.

"If you thought you were carrying his child, then perhaps you should tell him you're ill."

"I don't want to. I didn't want to tell you guys, remember?"

"Oh, I remember." I still had tile marks mashed into my butt, for God's sake.

"It's like—it's not real if nobody alive knows. Right?" She smiled crookedly, dark eyes filling with tears. "It's not happening to me if the only people who know are dead."

I felt like a total toad, watching her cry. "Come on, don't do that." I hugged her. Had she lost weight? Was she bonier than usual? I was embarrassed that I didn't know. And why hadn't *I* smelled anything different? Sure I was still rather new at this, but couldn't I learn stuff like that? Was I that damned selfish? So wrapped up in my own troubles that I didn't care when my best friend caught cancer?

And hey, *could* you catch cancer? I didn't know a thing about it. That would change as soon as I could get my ass to a computer. Or my hands on those seven fucking specialists.

"You're living with the king and queen of the vampires, a werewolf, an actor, *and* a doctor."

"And a Libra," Tina piped up, a rare joke.

"Right. We'll help you. We'll fix it."

"You're an idiot," Jessica sobbed in my arms.

"That's the spirit!"

"I'm sorry I didn't tell you," she finally offered. *Finally.* "It's just all this stuff with Sophie and Liam and Alonzo. And your birthday and your wedding. I didn't want to be the downer, you know?"

I knew. And that's when I got my idea. My really, ridiculously, atrociously bad idea.

CHAPTER 12

Sinclair and I were walking up Hennepin Avenue. The cops had done a great job lately in cleaning up the neighborhood; but you could still find trouble if you knew where to look. Minneapolis wasn't Cannon Falls, after all. It was still an American city with a nightlife.

"I know what you're thinking," he said at last.

"Prob'ly," I said, staring at the surprisingly clean gutter. I was profoundly bummed out. Myeloma—technically cancer of the bone marrow, and the blood plasma cells there—was serious. My research had been a total downer.

It could infect everything, and it carried with it fun symptoms like fatigue, pain, dehydration, constipation, susceptibility to infection, and even—ding, ding, ding!—kidney damage.

The good news was, Jessica's cancer was slow, which gave her and her doctor—and me—time to figure out options.

But right now, I could only come up with one.

"You're thinking of turning her."

"I'm still getting over the shock of finding out she's sick.

How come you didn't say anything?"

"It wasn't my secret to tell," he replied simply.

"I really hate you sometimes."

He didn't say anything.

"I just—I can't lose her. My best friend! I mean, I always knew, since I'm immortal and she's not, that it was a problem I'd have to face. But not *now*. She's only thirty, for God's sake!"

"Young," he agreed.

"I'm not ready to have this happen *now*. And I don't want her to be sick at all. Maybe—maybe I can fix it."

"And maybe you do your friend a disservice," he said quietly. "Maybe you should let her solve her own problems."

"Not knowing what to wear on a date is a *problem,* pal. This is a fucking *disaster*."

"This week has certainly had its twists and turns."

"Oh, boy, don't get me started." We walked along, headed toward burned-out streetlights. "How would I even do it?" I asked. "I've never made a vampire before. Hell, I'm trying to get off the whole blood-drinking thing entirely."

"Which is why we're walking down Hennepin at two A.M.," Sinclair pointed out. "As opposed to being home."

To get back at him for not giving me a heads-up about Jessica's *fucking fatal illness,* I'd told him about my zero blood diet. He'd taken it pretty well, but I knew why.

He didn't think I could do it.

He couldn't do it, which was why we were out prowling in the wee hours.

The scene when I'd told Sinclair about my new "no blood all the time" slim-down plan (does OB negative running down my chin make me look fat?) had been, like all the dramatic scenes in my life, anticlimactic.

We'd been necking in the shower and he'd moved in for a bite and I'd avoided him so deftly I nearly went ass over teakettle. He'd had to grab me to keep me from plunging through the shower curtain like Janet Leigh.

"What in the world . . . ?"

"Don't do that."

"As you wish." He'd let go. Then grabbed me again when I slipped again.

"I think we'd better rinse off before I kill myself."

He was standing under the shower, blinking water out of his eyes and staring down at me. "What is the matter, Elizabeth?"

"Nothing. Nothing! Uh. Nothing."

He hummed and looked at the ceiling.

"We're going to be in the shower until I spill it, aren't you?"

"In a manner of speaking."

If I'd been alive, I would have taken a deep, steadying breath. Instead, I counted backward from five, but by the time I was down to two, I couldn't wait any longer. Besides, the water was going to get cold any second. "I'm giving up blood drinking for my birthday."

"Giving up."

"Yeah."

"For your birthday."

"Yeah."

He rubbed his chin and I realized I had never seen Sinclair shave. Did vampires grow beards? I hoped not. Blech.

"No more victimizing would-be rapists?" he finally said. I could tell he was hoping that would be the end of it.

"No more at all. I mean, I'm the queen, right? There's perks, right?"

"Perks."

"Don't say 'perks' like there's a roach crawling around on your gums. Yeah, perks! And I figure, if I'm this all-powerful kick-ass queen you and Tina keep babbling about—"

"I never babble."

"—I should be able to decide when and where I drink blood."

"True."

"Or *if* I drink blood."

"Ah." He peered at me closely, almost as if seeing me for the first time. Except he looked at me like that at least twice a week. It was nice, if odd. Nobody in the world looked at me like that. "Are you the queen of the vampires if you don't drink blood?"

"If a tree falls in the forest and no one's around, does it squick you out by sucking out a hiker's blood? Come on, it's not that big a deal. Right? I mean, you know I'm nuts about you. It's not personal. In fact, it has nothing to do with you."

"Nothing to do with me," he parroted.

"Look, don't be like this, okay? I'm sorry, I shouldn't have picked the next time you wanted a chomp to tell you the feed store is closed, but there's been a ton of stuff going on." I reached out and wiped soap off his shoulders. His broad, broad shoulers. *Stay focused, idiot.* "You know I love everything we do in bed. And out of bed. And in the shower. And in the parlors. And—well, I adore every second of it. But I really need to do this. I still don't feel like drinking blood is part of who I am, so . . . so I'm not going to do it."

"You have shampoo on your ear," he informed me, and that was the last he'd said on the subject.

Now here we were, stalking prey for him.

Personally, I'd rather be back in the shower.

"So what's it like? Making a vampire?"

"Anticlimactic."

"Mister? Could you give me a hand?"

"Here we go," I muttered. Well dressed as we were, we must have looked like pigeons ready to be plucked.

She was tall, with dyed black hair. Torn stockings. Thin as a two-by-four. No coat, the better to see your boobs with, my dear. Her arms looked like windshield wipers.

"Yes, miss? Do you require assistance?" Sinclair let her get close.

"No," she replied, and I heard the pop of the switchblade. "I need your wallet."

"There are shelters and counselors available to help you," he informed her.

Her pimp was already flanking us in order to take us by surprise (so he thought), and as he made his move I back-handed him without even looking. It was easy. He spun and crashed to the ground.

Meanwhile, Sinclair had relieved the "professional" of her knife, picked her up so her feet dangled above the cracked sidewalk, and sank his teeth into her throat. She squealed and kicked, but I knew from experience it was like trying to get free from a tree.

I felt my own fangs pop out and had to look away.

I could (maybe) give up blood; Sinclair could not. But taking blood was downright sexual for us, so we'd compromised: we'd go out together. One-night stands only for him.

Did I like it? I did not. I fucking hated it. I should be the one he was growling over, the one in his arms. By choice, I was not. But I felt like a pimp.

He pulled free and her head lolled against his shoulder. He

looked at me with a vicious gleam in his eyes, blood staining
his grin. "Like some? There's plenty."

*Yes! Hand her over! No, hell with her, bite me now, and I'll
bite you, and that's how it'll be for a thousand years . . .*

"Let her go."

He dropped her. "As you wish." He bent, tucked a business
card from the nearest shelter into her top, straightened. Licked
his teeth. "Ummm. She needs more fatty acids in her diet. And
less crack. Shall we go?"

I shivered. "Eric, I love you, but sometimes you give me
such a case of the creeps."

He smiled at me. "Good."

CHAPTER 13

We took our bloodlust straight to the downtown Marriott, where Sinclair, the sneaky bastard, had booked a room. We'd barely made it through the door when we started tearing off our clothes, groping, kissing, sucking—everything but biting. And God, it was hard. It was like jerking off and not letting yourself come. Why, why, why was I doing this?

Because I would not be ruled by my fiendish bloodlust. I was the queen; it had to count for something. I was my own person, not a slave to my hungers.

I managed to keep those coherent thoughts until Sinclair tossed me on the bed, ripped through my skirt and panties, pushed my legs apart, and stuck his tongue inside me. I wrapped my legs around his neck and rode his mouth, both of us clawing through the bedspread. Then he was rearing over me, holding me apart with trembling fingers as he rammed into me with no finesse whatsoever. I didn't hold it against him.

O Elizabeth you queen you brat you darling

"Back atcha," I groaned while he pumped and worked

between my legs, while I bit my own lip so I wouldn't bite him, wouldn't eat him like the wolf ate Red Riding Hood.

Another weird queen thing: I could read Eric's mind during sex. He couldn't read mine. Yeah, that had gone over well. I'd finally told him, at the worst possible time, but the good news was, he hadn't had the worst possible reaction. We'd patched things up, but it hadn't been easy.

I can't believe I'm going along with your stupid bid for independence I should have you over my knee this minute

"Later," I panted. "You can spank me later."

I will you brat you lovely you darling

I yelled at the ceiling as I came, yelled and clutched at him and tried to pull him further into myself. He slid his hands beneath my ass and pinched me viciously as he shuddered into orgasm.

"Owwwww."

He rested his forehead on mine for a long moment.

"What was that for?" I bitched. To hell with afterglow.

"You deserve that and worse," he said, rolling off me. "Cutting me off from my favorite blood source. Why don't you take my testicles while you're at it?"

"Stop whining. If you really minded, there wouldn't be a thing *I* could do about it."

He smiled thinly, and contemplated the ruin of our clothes. "You really think so, don't you, darling?"

"What are you bitching about? You got fed, you got laid. No baby in sight. The whole night in front of us—alone."

The smile came again, a little more real this time. "Sometimes," he said, "you almost make sense."

"Yeah, well, sometimes I have panties on. What'd you do, eat them? There's scraps of clothing all over the place."

"I took the liberty of packing a bag."

"Well, thank goodness. You didn't, uh, *like* that whore, did you?"

He pulled me on top of him and suddenly I was looking into his black eyes, which, since I had just been looking around for my underpants, was startling. "You know my heart and my soul," he said quietly, tenderly. "You can read my mind, something no one else on the planet can do. There is. No. Comparison." He shook me a little at each word to make his point. "Though I must say I find your insecurity quite charming."

"Shut up. I'm sorry to make you drink from strange women—"

"*I* don't mind," he said silkily.

"—it's just something I have to do for myself, you know? Not drink, I mean. I know it seems dumb to you—what'd you call it? My stupid bid for independence? If I was you, I'd probably think it was dumb, too. But it just seems—this whole past year—like I've been on a ride I can't get off. This is something I can control. I'm sorry if it screws you over." To my surprise, I suddenly felt like crying.

He hugged me to him. "Darling, don't do that. I know what it's like to be a slave to the thirst. I think what you do is wondrous. I'll support you as long as you—"

"Can hold out?"

"—decide to stay with this course of action," he corrected himself.

"Thanks. For a puke, you can be pretty nice sometimes."

"Crumbs from the lady's table," he said with grim good humor, and got up to find the overnight bag.

Later, we made love again, slowly and tenderly, sliding

against each other and purring like the big predators we were. And for a whole night, I didn't think about BabyJon or Sophie or Alonzo, or even Jessica.

CHAPTER 14

"There's a zombie in the attic," Cathie said, and I nearly yakked up my gum. She was a ghost—literally, the spirit of a dead person—and as she spoke she floated through the wall, into my bedroom. Cathie had been a tall woman, almost as tall as me, with honey-tinted hair pulled back in a perpetual pony-tail, a green sweatshirt, and black stretch pants. Barefoot. For eternity! At least her feet were attractive. They were little and pretty, with unpolished but nicely shaped toenails.

"This is no time for your quirky sense of humor," I snapped as I lugged a pile of near-empty journals into my closet. It never failed—I'd buy a new journal, write like a madwoman for ten pages, then lose total interest in the process. Three months later, I'd start the whole process all over again. I think I just liked buying new notebooks.

"Well, well! You seem touchy! What's the matter, didn't get laid last night?"

It was scary how much she sounded like me sometimes. Maybe that's why she totally got on my nerves. "That's not the problem at all. I just hate it when you dart out of solid walls to tell me ridiculous stories."

"Well, it's not like I have a choice," she said crossly, floating through my bathroom door and then back out again. "After all, the shortest distance between two points is a straight line. You'd walk through walls, too, if you could. And it's not like I can ring a doorbell to get your attention. As for the zombie—is it my fault you're in denial about reanimated corpses?"

"*I'm* a reanimated corpse," I said glumly. "Let me deal with that. There's no such thing as zombies anyway."

Cathie stuck her head into the wall (probably just to creep me out, since she knew it drove me crazy), pulled it back out, and said, "Why do I bother?" and stuck it back in. "Where is everybody?"

"Sinclair isn't up yet, ditto Tina, Jessica's at an appointment, Marc's at work, Toni and Garrett haven't left her bedroom since she got back, and I *was* enjoying my privacy."

"Too bad. I'm bored, and you guys are exciting company."

She'd been killed by a serial killer a few months ago, and come to me for help. Unlike other ghosts who came to me for help, once she got what she wanted, she stayed. I wasn't a vampire queen, I was a damn soul collector. Nobody left; they all just chained themselves to me like eternal chattel. But they were all too fucking sassy for the phenomenon to be flattering.

"I bring good news from the underworld," she was booming in a terrible Vincent Price imitation. "All's quiet on the Midwestern Front."

"Yeah?"

"Well, there have been ghosts, but I've been helping them."

"You've been helping ghosts who seek my favor, without even telling me? So you're like my—"

"You know those Hollywood assistants who handle all the producer's problems so she can concentrate on making movies? That's what I do now. I help the little people."

"You want to make movies?" She had lost me. And so soon in the conversation, too.

"No, dumb shit, I'm like the assistant who tends to the little people."

I felt my eyes bulge. "I don't think you should call them that."

"I'm doing you a favor, okay? Usually these ghosts just want someone to listen, maybe point them in the right direction. You've got higher priorities right now, I gather."

"Well, thanks." I must not have sounded convincing, because she glared at me. "No, really. Thanks. The last thing I need this week is another needy ghost dropping by for favors."

"You're welcome. It's actually kind of nice. They can see me and talk to me, just like you. I mean, look at my options! I have to talk to you, or I can talk to them."

"Well, you've made the right choice," I said with faux enthusiasm.

"Don't get too down. At least your hot, hunky boyfriend can see you and touch you. Your friends can see and touch you. What have I got? A distracted vampire with a long to-do list ahead of me and my problems."

"Cathie, that's not true!" I couldn't believe I was getting a lecture from a woman in a green sweatshirt. "I solved your problem right away, didn't I? The bad guy's dead, if memory serves."

"Yeah," she said, cheering up. "Your sister cracked his head open like an egg."

"So what do you want from me now?"

"I dunno. But there's got to be more than *this*." She sulkily floated through the wall.

"Tell me about it!" I shouted after her.

CHAPTER 15

Because things weren't awful enough, an hour later Marjorie the scary librarian popped by and chimed the bell. I put my foot down: no. Just because people—

"Very old, very powerful vampires," Sinclair interrupted.

—stopped by without proper planning or scheduling—

"She says it's an emergency. You want her to plan her emergencies?"

—didn't mean I had to drop everything and rush to the parlor.

"No one was in the parlor," Marjorie announced, pushing open the swinging door into the kitchen, "so I let myself in."

Tina followed closely on the librarian's heels with a pained, helpless expression. I gave Sinclair a look.

"Ah," he began. "Marjorie. So good to see you again. But perhaps now—"

"Majesty," the elder vampire said, dipping her head. "Very rude to barge in, I know; but what I have is extremely important."

"Of course it is," I sighed. "A nice new crisis you're gonna drop in my lap."

"Are you suggesting, Majesty, that I should let all important matters run their course without your intervention?" She smiled a little and fiddled with her sweater cuffs.

No, just call first.

Marjorie looked around the kitchen approvingly. The big wooden table in the center had plenty of chairs for all of us. More than enough to hold Sinclair, Tina, Jessica, and me. Everybody else was—heck, I didn't know, what was I, the fucking family calendar?

Marjorie was a severe-looking woman of ordinary height, dark hair with gray wings at the temples, and sensible shoes. She ran the vampire library in the warehouse district—the biggest, I had been told, in the Midwest.

She tried to keep tabs on all vampires, recently turned or otherwise, kept their mortgages and bills paid up (in the case of new vampires, that was especially nice . . . if they ever came back to themselves they would find a home and their credit rate unaltered), kept nice neat computer files (or, in earlier ages, carefully maintained paper files) on everyone she could. How *did* she do that? No one knew.

Anyway, she had been around before Nostro's time (Nostro = deceased disgusting despot), and before Nostro's sire's time, too. She had little interest in explicit displays of power, which was probably good news for the rest of us. Just stayed in her library, organizing lives, collecting a different sort of power—one that wasn't so intrusive, but nevertheless caught our attention when gently applied.

Anyway, she had that look of relieved approval because she saw a traditional scene that must have warmed her heart: the king and queen, with lackey (Tina) in attendance, with presumed blood-sheep (Marc and Jessica) close at hand.

"Nice to see you again, Dr. Spangler," she said, since I wasn't re-introducing her to anybody.

"Hi, uh—sorry, I—"

"Marjorie."

"Right." He'd been heads together with Jessica until a few seconds ago, but now he was looking downright flustered. Marjorie had that effect on humans. She could snap her fingers and Marc or Jess would have obediently opened a vein. "Nice to see you again."

"Thank you."

A short silence followed while Marjorie waited for us to dismiss the peons.

"So," I said before Eric could speak, because he actually *would* have dismissed the peons, "what brings you to Summit Avenue?"

"This," she said, whipping out—a gun! A knife! A brick!

No, my nerves were just a little overwrought. It was—

Tina frowned, causing a neat wrinkle to form between her eyes. It made her look positively ancient—twenty-five instead of her usual eighteen. "That's a book catalog."

"Correct."

"Thank all that is holy and unholy," I proclaimed with even less patience than usual, "that you didn't waste a second getting this over here! Why, we've been combing this entire mansion, top to bottom, for a book catalog. Our need has never been more dire."

"Specifically," Marjorie said, slapping it down on the table, "it's the Berkley Fall Catalog for this year."

Sinclair closed his eyes.

"Yes, well that is the Holy Grail of book catalogs," I said, still walking the line between playing along and suggesting to this woman that she leave before my head exploded.

Sinclair didn't say anything, but his grim look and slight shake of the head suggested he knew where this was going.

I didn't. Marjorie waited for me to catch on. I quietly trusted she had packed a lunch. Finally, she said, "Page forty-seven."

Nobody moved. Apparently she was talking to me. I picked up the slick catalogue and thumbed to the appropriate page. And nearly dropped it like it had turned into a rattler. "Okay, I can see why you might think this is . . ."

"A catastrophe?" she said sharply.

". . . bad. A little bit bad."

Undead and Unwed by Anonymous was splashed across a two-page spread. *Hilarious new take on the vampire genre!* was printed across the bottom, along with other critical comments ("abrupt transitions make for a rollicking ride all the same" and "low on plot but high on fun!").

There was also a quick paragraph: "Playing along with the 'true autobiography' approach, the author poses the clever conceit of suggesting herself queen of the mythical undead. One of the fall's brightest!"

"Somebody wrote a book about you?" Jessica asked, staring at the catalog spread. "Wow!"

"Not wow. The opposite of wow." *What would that be,* I asked myself wildly. *It's not like you can just spell it backward and hope that works. Maybe invert it—owo? As in, "owo is me"?*

"Majesties. I don't question your judgment—"

"But you're going to."

Marjorie looked as anxious as I'd ever seen her. "How could you let this happen?"

"It was—" *A favor for a friend,* I started to say, but Sinclair stepped on that in a hurry.

"Can the book be pulled?"

"It's not *our* book," she pointed out, sounding pissed. "You may as well ask if the new Stephen King can be pulled—we had nothing to do with it."

"*Can* the new Stephen King be pulled?" Marc joked. He was an "old-school" King snob—nothing good since *Pet Sematary,* he once claimed. I kept buying them, though. Letting go of King was like letting go of your favorite greasy spoon hangout. You don't. They're still open, so you keep going, out of pure love and memory of the good old days.

I looked at the spread again. Dark blue cover, silver lettering. "The first true tale from the undead trenches." Sure.

I knew who had written it: Jon Delk, formerly of the vampire-hunting Blade Warriors, current hot author. Not that he knew it—thanks to a bit of quick memory wiping.

Of course, the source *behind* the author had been me.

A few months ago, Jon had come by to talk me out of marrying Sinclair. A college student by day and ferocious vampire hunter by night, he'd sworn off the stake a few months ago. Meeting me had made him see a whole new side to vampires, I gathered. These days he and the rest of his little Cub Scout den from hell asked questions first and staked later.

Grateful for Delk's change of heart, I'd told him my story, which he used for a college paper. Then the manuscript disappeared, and Sinclair made Jon forget he'd written it. Problem solved. Right?

A fresh new take on the vampire tale from someone who's actually been there, according to *Publishers Weekly*.

"Jon's gonna be pissed," I said, shaking my head.

"Only if we tell him."

"Of course we're gonna tell him! We can't not tell him. That would be—"

"The feelings of the infant who wrote this are the least of your problem," Marjorie pointed out sharply. "I can assure you, the vampire community will not be happy about this. We have spent a millennium in hiding; you've been in power for about year, and now—"

"Charming anti–Anne Rice tale from a vampire with real world problems!" Marc read helpfully.

"We need to deal with this now," Sinclair said quickly. "If we cannot stop the book's publication—"

"What's the spin?" I asked.

"Do you even need any?" Jessica asked. She looked a little like a cornered mouse when we all stared at her, then spoke up again. "Nobody's going to think there are *really* vampires running around. I mean, look at this ad. If you were reading it, would your first thought be, *oh my gosh, this is real, cover the kids in garlic and sprinkle the doorstep with holy water?* No way. It's obvious that it's a fiction book pretending to be nonfiction."

"Except," Marc said, "it's nonfiction pretending to be fiction."

"Right, but what live human being—other than the very few of us who already know—will realize that? Of course, if you try to get the book pulled, that really *will* get people interested. Who's trying to stop this book? Why? Are they a satanic cult? Do they worship vampire mythology?" She paused for dramatic effect. "Then: why do they act like vampires? Do they really think they are? And wow, why don't any of them have suntans?"

Marjorie leaned forward and whispered in Sinclair's ear. He nodded.

"What? What was that? Don't keep secrets. Are you keeping secrets? Marjorie, don't you know the whole 'share it with the class' rule?" I said.

"I was only asking," she said, "if your friend knew she was ill, and I was speaking privately because it was off the topic, and I didn't wish you to think I wasn't paying attention."

"Thanks, but I did know," Jessica said. She even smiled. Marjorie didn't, and I realized Jessica had made a classic mistake where vampires were concerned. Marjorie may have sniffed out Jessica's cancer, but she didn't give a shit if this specific blood-sheep ever recovered. She was just curious about Eric's feeding habits.

"Getting back to business," Tina said. "I think Jessica makes an excellent point. Trying to restrain a book only increases its impact."

"Very well," Marjorie said. "I only wished to bring this to your attention. What you do with this information is entirely up to you."

"Somebody better bring it to *Jon's* attention," I muttered, closing the catalog and trying to hand it back.

She gave me a chilly smile. "No, thank you, Majesty. I have plenty of copies."

"Well, thanks for bring that extra special bit of fun into our lives," I said back, with equal warmth. Which was to say, with no warmth.

"Any excuse to spend extra time with Your Majesty."

"I'll see you out," Tina said, rising and gesturing to the door.

"Thank you," Sinclair said politely, staring down at the catalog with a thin twist of his mouth, "for stopping by."

"Yeah, thanks loads."

"Majesties. Dr. Spangler. Miss." And off she went, ready to spread more joy to other vampire households.

———

CHAPTER 16

"There is a book about you?" Alonzo asked, his dark Spanish eyes aglow.

More pop-ins! Oh, wait. It was possible Tina had mentioned the Europeans had scheduled another meeting. At least we were in one of the parlors this time, instead of being ambushed in the kitchen by bitchy librarians. In fact, this was my favorite parlor (who knew I'd ever live in a house where I'd have a favorite parlor?), with the cheerful candy-striped wallpaper and blonde wood furniture. Big east-facing windows let in tons of natural light (I assumed), and the room was heated by a gorgeous, midnight blue ceramic stove in the corner.

I was beginning to feel like I was spending half my (new) life in parlors. Thank heavens we had four, or I would get bored with the wallpaper. Now the idea of opulent mansions suddenly made sense.

"Really and truly," I answered Alonzo. "Look: we only told you guys so you wouldn't freak out if you, you know, happened to be in Barnes and Noble looking for some light reading before you iced the girl at the coffee counter."

"I appreciate the genuine concern in your otherwise need-lessly provocative statement," Alonzo said. He shot his cuffs and looked at his watch, a big chunky silver thing that looked like it weighed down his wrist. He did it so often I assumed it was some sort of tic.

"Provoke this," I retorted.

"The book is not quite out yet," Sinclair pointed out, clinging to hope like a balding man with a sparse comb-over.

"Yes, it's a bright new fall offering," I added. "Place your orders now. Beat the rush!"

"I'd like to beat *you,*" Sinclair muttered, which I didn't think was very unifying of him. Then, louder, he added, "We are, as you say, keeping you in the loop."

In fact, there had been a wicked big argument about it. My initial take was, let them read about it on the *New York Times* bestseller list. Who cares about their feelings? I mean, Gawd. Look at the sitch. We've got bigger problems than a book about my alleged (what was the opposite of alleged?) life story. Like Jessica being *deathly friggin' ill.* Sophie needing revenge. The Europeans needing to kick me out and take over. Maybe on that last one; it was possible they only needed to clear customs on the way home. Anyway, a book nobody would think was true was the least of my problems.

Tina and Sinclair were adamantly opposed to my own supe-rior point of view. Like parrots playing off each other, they kept telling me in grating and repetitive ways that it was better to tell these Europeans about the book before they found out themselves and used our silence. Use it how, they didn't elab-orate.

Anyway, since my number one complaint about being dead

was that nobody told me anything, I eventually agreed to let Alonzo and the others know. For once, *I'd* called the meeting (well, Tina had called for me). For once, *I* was expecting company. Yeah! How 'bout *that*?

"I confess," Alonzo was saying, "I have no idea what to say. This is an unusual problem." He gave me an admiring look.

"Listen, totally off the subject, can I ask you something?"

"Majesty, I am at your disposal."

Now was the perfect opportunity. Jessica was asleep—or, at least, in her room. Marc was working. It was just us dead people.

"What's it like, to make a vampire?"

"Oh, well." Alonzo looked uncharacteristically flustered, and ran a hand over his smooth head. "I never, ah, stayed to take care of one. That is to say—"

"You always chomped and moved on."

"Would you ask a lion to sit with the corpse of the gazelle, as the hyenas and vultures tore at the tendons?"

"People aren't gazelles," I pointed out, restraining my temper with some difficulty. *You brought it up, you brought it up.* "So there might be other vampires running around, ones you made?"

"It is likely," he said reluctantly. "In my youth. Now, of course, I have much more control over the thirst."

"See, I avoid that whole thing by not even drinking. You should try it!"

"This, what you say, 'avoid the whole thing.' This is physically impossible." Frustration, intrigue, admiration, and rage crossed his features all at once. It made his eyes go really squinty and he was rubbing his head so much I wondered if he was trying to start a fire up there.

"Feeding leads to killing. It happens time and time again,

vampire after vampire. I can't even imagine," I said, speaking more to myself than anyone in the room. "Killing somebody. I mean—"

Okay, I had killed someone. Two someones. Wait, four, if you counted vampires. Hmmm, official Gray Area ahead. But they were all self-defense, right? And the vampires were already dead, right? Neither of which Alonzo could claim about Sophie.

"Walk with me?" the Spaniard asked, getting up smoothly from his spot on the love seat.

"Yeah," I said, standing up an instant later. "Sure. No problem."

Sinclair raised his eyebrows at me, but didn't say a word or make a move.

So we went.

We'd put our coats on; he had put back on the slightly muddy but still meticulously crafted black wingtips he had left in the hallway upon his entrance. For myself, I'd slipped into a somewhat fashionable pair of bright red rubber boots—it was wet out. Spring in Minnesota meant thaw, and thaw meant mud.

"At last," he teased when we had walked a block without saying anything to each other. "I have spirited you away from the king."

"Yeah. I don't even know why we're talking. I sort of thought when I first met you, that we'd end up at each other's throats. You know, after Sophie had her turn."

"Have you decided what to do with me?"

I nearly walked into a melting snowbank. "Seriously? You're asking me?"

"I am but a loyal subject. Your will is my will."

"I appreciate the thought." And, weirdly, I did. "Is it real? I mean, is it genuine? If I said, 'Okay, Alonzo, I'm going to cut off your head because you were a bad vampire a hundred years ago,' you'd just go along with it?"

"Well," he admitted, neatly avoiding a sample of thawing dog poo that had likely been there since January, "I wouldn't calmly kneel before you and wait for the sword to swing, but I respect the power of the monarchy."

"In other words, you don't think I'd be so cruel."

"No," he replied. "I don't think you would be so cruel. In fact, I am counting on it."

"You really don't think I'd do anything to you?"

His words came out with careful measure. "That would be an overstatement. I do not think you would kill me in cold blood."

Well, nuts.

"It would be easier," I said with a sigh, "if you and your friends were the bloodthirsty monsters I thought you were at first. Maybe the six of you could leave town in a trail of blood. Then killing would be easy."

"This should not concern the others," he said emphatically. "This is a matter between me and Dr. Trudeau. And your Majesty, of course."

"Is that why you came over tonight by yourself?"

"You only sent for me."

"You're the only one whose name I can remember," I admitted, and he laughed.

In the distance, I could hear barking and yowling and toenails clicking on sidewalk. I figured we had about two more minutes before all the neighborhood dogs descended. There was a reason I didn't like taking walks.

"Let's head back."

"We only just—"

"Dude, trust me. You do not want to be here five minutes from now. We can talk more in the garden behind the mansion. Behind the fence."

He obediently turned with me as I did a one-eighty and started heading back up the sidewalk to the house. He was right; it was a little silly. We were barely out of the shadow of the mansion. I had barely talked to him about anything. Wait— had it been my idea to go for a walk? I tried to remember. No. He'd asked me.

"I have another question for you, Majesty."

"Oh, great. My turn again. Except we're not playing a game."

"About that, *señorita,* you are wrong. But here is my question: are you going to turn your friend into a vampire? Or wait for her to die and bury her and mourn her?"

"How do you even *know* about that?"

"You mean, before you asked me what it was like to make a vampire? I guessed. I know she is ill, and after seeing you and her in the same room, I could make some assumptions."

The mansion loomed larger before us, the dark and forlorn branches of surrounding trees still waiting for rebirth. The baying of dogs was coming closer.

He broke the silence again. "You do not seem the type of lady to give up her friends so very easily."

I chewed on that one for a moment. The thing about Alonzo was, even when he said something nice, it wasn't like he was sucking up. Maybe it was in the translation of his ideas from Spanish to English; but his well-crafted words betrayed a certain attention for my well-being. In fact, he made for a pleasant change from most vampires here in America, who either (a) ignored me or (b) tried to kill me.

"I only just found out my friend was sick," I said finally. "I don't know what I'm going to do, yet."

"I beg your pardon. But I believe you do."

We stopped together at the iron gate on the west side of the house. It led to the brown and lifeless gardens behind the house. But neither of us reached for the latch. Instead, we watched each other for several seconds. *Game indeed,* I thought.

"Well," I said finally, "you're assuming my friend will even go along with it."

"She has a choice?"

"If she didn't, she wouldn't really be my *friend,* would she?"

"Your uniqueness," he offered, "is both blessing and a curse. Blessing, in that you are different from others, which I always see as a positive. A curse, in that you generate problems of your own making—problems that vampires like me do not trouble with."

"For example?"

"I have never known a vampire to remain friends with a human—certainly not long enough to consider a careful plan to turn that friend."

"Never? And you've been around, what? A hundred years? Two hundred? And in that time, you've never made a friend and then wanted to keep them around?" My situation with Jessica couldn't have been that out there . . . and neither could Sophie and Liam's.

"Not a living human," he answered with arms stretched and palms up. "And when you generate two estimates of my age, you would do well to round to the higher one." One of the hands lifted higher than the other.

I laughed.

"There's us," he said, finally swinging opening the gate and entering the garden, "and there are them. The two cannot mix. No good comes of this. Your situation—forgive my boldness, Your Majesty—I see your situation as the inevitable, and unfortunate, end result of your unreasonable attachment to your human friends. Someday, you will end up in the same place with your doctor friend. Each of these endings will devastate you, weaken you—and to no good purpose."

"I don't see it that way at all." I felt a little defensive, but also grateful to this vampire. Which was amazing in and of itself. But Alonzo was giving me the first chance I had really had to organize my thoughts. A rare and wonderful thing, in my case.

"How do you see it, my queen?"

My thoughts assembled rapidly as I said the words, and I felt more secure in my opinion with each new idea. "I gain strength from my friends, not weakness. My 'situation' with Jessica is not the 'end result' of anything. It's a step in our journey together. Maybe she dies, maybe she lives. But she is an essential part of me, either way. What am I without these friends?

"Faster, stronger, generally superior," he suggested.

"Superior," I muttered. "I'm afraid I don't like that word very much. Especially when vampires use it."

"Oh dear." He gave a knowing smile as he walked beside me on the dead garden path. The baying of the dogs faltered in the distance. "No wonder you had a problem with the former regime."

CHAPTER 17

We slipped into the back entrance of the house and just sort of stood around for a moment in the mudroom. I wanted to go to the kitchen and hang out with Jessica for a while—give her a chance to maybe tell me how the doctor's appointments were going. How everything was going. The thing about Jess— you couldn't force information out of her. She'd tell you or she wouldn't. I planned to make the atmosphere as welcoming as I could.

Anyway, I was pretty much done with Alonzo. I'm sure he was done with me. And Sinclair wasn't the "hey, let's go play golf in the dark" kind of guy. In fact, I had never seen Sinclair with one man friend. In further fact, as far as I knew, Tina was his only friend.

Anyway, Sinclair was done with Alonzo. Tina wasn't even there—she was tracking Jon down for us.

So it was that part of the party where you want your friends to leave, and they want to leave, but it was too early to look at your watches.

"It's getting late," Alonzo said, stealing another glance at his big silver watch. *Thank God!* Normally that weird tic of his made me wonder if a bomb was set to go off somewhere. But this time I welcomed it. "And unlike some, I must feed before dawn. With your permission, Majesty . . . ?"

"Of course. Um, try not to kill your food." I tried to say it as a joke, but it probably sounded like an order. Enough—I was too emotionally exhausted to try to explain. Let him figure it out. "Thanks for coming over."

"The pleasure was mine." He smiled at me, showing me how very pleased he was. "I was waiting and waiting for the phone to ring. And now, I will go back and wait some more."

"Hmmmph." I was 98 percent sure he was fucking with me, but he had enough slipperiness in his tone that just made it quicker to repeat, as I did, "Thanks for coming over."

He went. I listened for Sinclair but he didn't pop out from a hidden shadow the way he usually did. Nobody was pulling up in the drive. Tina was standing unobtrusively in the short hall to the kitchen, ready to spring forward with a cup of tea.

I slung my coat into the mudroom closet, kicked off my boots, and made for the kitchen.

Sinclair was there, sitting with Marc and Jessica and reading Sun Tzu's *The Art of War*. His sleeves were rolled up. His feet were bare. He looked as comfy as ever.

Not that I wanted him breathing down my neck, but . . .

"Shouldn't you be, uh, waiting breathlessly to hear about my walk with Alonzo? Did he swear allegiance? Did he bone me at the intersection with Dale Avenue?"

"Oh." He turned a page. "About the first, Alonzo is gradually falling under your spell."

"My spell?"

He looked at me innocently. "Why, dear, your natural charm. No doubt you had it before you were a vampire queen; but it's all the stronger now. No one of any intelligence can resist you for long."

See, there it was again, just like Alonzo—the 98 percent certainty that this guy was just fucking with me. I just waved a hand and let him continue.

"I only have to wait a few more days, and then he will be yours and, by association, ours. As for the latter, if you wanted to use your walk to, ah, show carnal interest, there is nothing I can do about it. And if you bit him, or allowed him to bite you—"

"Fat goddamned chance."

"Yes, well." He shrugged. "I was not especially worried."

"Okay, there's got to be something between total disinterest and hanging all over me. This"—I gestured—"isn't it. But anyway, even though you seem, uh, not too worried about it, I'll tell you how the walk went."

"The walk with the guy who's going to fall in love with you?" Marc asked.

"He's *not* going to fall in love with me. Besides, I think he's—I mean, if he was going to fall in love with anybody— which he's not—look, can we stay on track, please?"

Just then I saw Marc slip Jessica something small and white—it looked like a business card—and whisper to her. I cut myself off. "What was that? Are you telling secrets? What did you tell her? *Share with the class!* Are you getting sicker? You're not getting sicker, are you?"

I couldn't smell *anything* different about her. Of course, I didn't exactly go out of my way to smell my girlfriend, so I didn't exactly have a baseline for comparison purposes. But still. You'd think I could tell something.

"Take a pill," Marc said. "I'll give you one. I was giving her the business card of a guy I want her to see. He's a really good doc—my dad saw him."

And is still alive, right? I was embarrassed to ask. I knew Marc's dad was sick, but surely I would have heard if he'd died. Somebody would have told me, right? We share with the class!

"How's your dad?"

"He's really good." Weirdly, Marc said this in an almost glum tone. "They got him in this new place, he likes it a lot. It's a real house, not a hospital or anything. He's one of a couple guys who lives there, and the nurse who owns the place keeps an eye on them, you know, makes sure they get their meds and see their docs, but she's not, you know, taking care of them in an obvious way. If he wants to retreat to his own space and watch a baseball game, he can. Or he can eat in the dining room if he wants company. It's a pretty good compromise."

"That's great." I said this with total sincerity. And it was, beyond obvious reasons: so, so great to hear good news for a change. "You should bring him by to—"

"Meet all my cool new vampire friends?" Jessica smothered a snicker as he continued. "Honey, he had a huge problem with my lifestyle when I was just gay. Now I'm gay and living with vampires."

"Well, it's not like you're sleeping with any of us." I shrugged.

"Hmm." His eyes searched the hallway behind me. "So, what's Alonzo's story? Did he go home? Is he sticking around? I just thought—"

"Alonzo's not an option, Marc. Honestly."

"Yeah, well. You never know. You know how it is. You're new in town, you don't know the good bars, you—"

"Go out and kill a waitress for the fun of it?"

"Still working through that?" Jessica asked.

"Well, no matter how we deal with it among vampires, I'm sure Marc can agree that murder is a really great reason not to date a guy, doy!"

"Oh, I dunno. That whole 'falling for the dark side' thing worked out kind of good for you," Marc said, his gaze sliding to Sinclair for a moment.

My mind went blank. A cliché I completely understood: I could feel my brain trying to make words and not coming up with a thing. Nothing. Empty. *Nada*. Finally I managed, "Do as I say, not as I do. And Eric's a good guy. When he kills in cold blood, he does it for a good reason. You know, like love in his heart."

"Ah, darling," Sinclair said, gaze on his book.

"And I know he's cute and all," Jessica said, "Alonzo, I mean, but I don't think he *dates*. You know, those types have minions and contemporaries, but I don't think there's much emotional attachment anywhere, with anyone."

"True," Sinclair said, still not looking up, "but do not discount Dr. Spangler's scruffy Gen-X charm."

"No, you don't," I said, ignoring how Marc suddenly looked pleased and puffed up a little. "I'm on to you, bud. You're not sneaking under Alonzo's radar by having one of us date him."

Shit, when Detective Nick asked Jessica out, Sinclair practically drove her to her date. He *loooved* the idea of a cop being on our little "go, vampires!" team.

"So he's headed back to the hotel?" Marc pressed.

"After a quick stop to commit felony assault," I said glumly.

"You two are getting so chummy," Jessica said, "I'm surprised he didn't ask you to go with him to rustle up some dinner."

"No thanks."

"You talked to Sophie's people lately?"

I slunk into one of the chairs. "What people? It's her, and it's Liam. And no. All's quiet from their end. They're waiting, I guess. For me. To do whatever."

Like Alonzo. Like all of us: stuck in the same web of waiting. If I could get my hands on the guy who made the web, I'd throttle him.

"So, what?" Jessica asked. "Did Alonzo try to jump your bones?"

"Or did a slobbering horde of golden retrievers descend on you before he could make his move?" Marc piped up.

"Shut up, shut up. He didn't make any moves. He didn't do anything. He asked me some stuff and I asked him some stuff. And then we came back."

"What 'stuff'?" Jessica asked, suspicion making her tone heavy.

Oh, whether or not I was going to put the chomp on you, nothing to worry about. "Vampire stuff," I said, and wouldn't say more, no matter how much she bugged me. Which, by the way, was a considerable amount.

CHAPTER 18

It was the next night and we were back in the kitchen. Half the table (and it was a big table) was covered with liquor bottles and half-full drinking glasses. It looked like we were all going on a bender, but the truth was, Marc was trying to teach us how to make rainbows.

Jessica was having a bit of success; she'd get her rainbow halfway made and then the grenadine would sort of squiggle into the rest of it.

All my rainbows looked like mud. I was so fucking thirsty I didn't care; I drank the mistakes. The real tragedy was, I didn't feel anything close to drunk.

"Just—okay, watch me again. See? You slooooowly let it sort of dribble off the spoon. Otherwise it'll all moosh together."

"I can get the first layer," I said, watching Marc (who had put himself through med school tending bars) carefully build a rainbow-colored drink of grenadine, vodka, that blue stuff that looked like Windex, sweet and sour mix, and something else I didn't know the name of. I wouldn't have wanted to drink it (well, I was drinking it, but if I were still alive these concoctions would have had me on my ass) but once Marc made it, it sure looked pretty. "Then it all goes to hell."

"Free booze and a metaphor for life, too!" Jessica watched her rainbow come apart, rushed it to her lips, and then made a face and put the glass down. "Why are we all learning how to make a drink none of us like to, um, drink?"

"I saw one of the bartenders at Scratch make one and thought it looked cool. Once I was sure one of the layers wasn't blood—"

mmmm, blood, precious blood

"—I thought it'd be fun to try. And I wasn't going to ask that vampire how to do it. She's fairly surly as a bartender, and worse when she's hostess."

Where had *that* come from? Actually, I was starting to think about blood a lot more and more. You know those cartoons when the wolf looks at his friends and they turn into rib roasts and stuff before his eyes?

Jess and Marc were starting to look *reeeally* good.

"Maybe if you were a little friendlier to the Scratch vampires," B-positive—I mean, Marc, began, "they'd treat you—"

"Look, nobody's trying to kill me right now and that's just fine. If they don't *like* me, that's just how it goes. I got over needing people to *like* me in tenth grade, when I spied the captain of the cheerleading squad on her knees in front of the offensive line of the football team under the bleachers, one day after school. I figured that wasn't the life for me."

"Of course," Jessica observed as she experimented with different rainbow colors, "she somehow still pulled off Miss Congeniality two years later."

"What was your secret, Betsy?" Marc's eyes glittered with a fascination. "Did you do the defensive line instead? I hear that's where all the votes are."

"Honey, you tell me. You probably blew more guys in high school than I did."

He laughed. "Miss Congeniality! Seriously, that's great! Do you still have the crown and sash? I could get a date in no time if you'd lend me those props for five minutes."

I drank another failed rainbow and ignored an empty bottle of vodka as it tumbled to the floor and rolled under the table. "Forget about it."

"Yeah, but just think—"

"Marc, I said fucking forget it, okay? Do I have get out the hand puppets? Knock it off!"

"Jeez, Betsy, I was only kidding around."

I resisted the urge to throw my empty glass at him. I wasn't mad at him. I wasn't mad at anybody. I was just . . .

Just really thirsty.

"I'm sorry," I said, not meaning it, but that was what people said in such circumstances. "I'm a little on edge these days."

"Sure, no problem. I had half your problems, I'd stress out, too."

Well you don't so why don't you SHUT THE FUCK UP?

"Uh-huh," I said brightly. The smell of all the booze was making me a little light-headed. Not to mention the smell of B-positive's aftershave. I probably shouldn't be drinking so much on an empty stomach. Not that I could get drunk. Well, maybe I could. Eventually.

"Yeah, uh, Betsy, we've been meaning to talk to you about this." This from myeloma. I was pretty sure I could smell it now.

"About what?"

"Your no blood-drinking thing."

"It's not a *thing,* it's a lifestyle. You know," I added brightly to Marc, "like yours. I'm *choosing* not to drink blood."

Marc almost dropped the grenadine. He turned to give me his full attention when Jessica jumped in with, "Nuh-uh! Picking a fight to get out of talking about this won't work."

"Right," Marc said, looking less convinced. "That won't work. Bitch."

Nuts. "Oh, come on, you guys!" I rested my forehead on the table. "I figured you'd be supportive."

"Supportive of you breaking Sinclair's heart and making yourself nuttier than you usually are? Honey, your temper these days is almost as bad as mine."

"Well, why don't you shut your fucking face, then?" I straightened up in a hurry as my vision cleared. "Sorry. That sort of slipped out."

"Great," Marc mumbled. "Vampire Tourette's syndrome."

"And Sinclair's heart isn't broken. And even if it was, it's none of your business."

"How's he supposed to feel when you tell him not only are you going on a hunger strike, he is, too, unless he cheats on you with other people?" Marc demanded.

"What part of 'none of your business' do you not get?"

"Ha!" Marc wiped off his lips and began refilling another glass with yet another perfect rainbow. "We have to live with you guys, you know."

"No," I said pointedly. "You don't."

"What's *that* supposed to mean?" Jessica asked.

I rubbed my eyebrows. "Nothing. It's not supposed to mean anything. Sinclair's heart isn't broken."

"He's been moping around this place like he heard yellow was the new black," she added.

"We worked that out. We have a plan for him getting his blood."

Marc snorted. "Yeah, I'm sure it's not awful."

I threw my hands in the air. "So, what? What are you telling me? Start drinking again? Hurt more people? Maybe kill someone by accident if I go too far?"

"What happened between Alonzo and Sophie won't necessarily happen to you."

"I *knoow,*" I said. I was a little astonished. One thing had nothing to do with the other. I had started my hunger strike way before Sophie even got to town. Right?

"Moderation," Marc was babbling. "Everything in moderation. Besides, aren't you the only vampire who only has to drink once or twice a week? How are you going to kill somebody doing that?"

"I plan," I said grimly, "on being the only vampire who doesn't have to drink at all."

"Well, it's making you nuts," Jessica snapped, "at the worst possible time for me. And if I find one more piece of chewing gum on the banister, I'm evicting you. I figure you've gone through twenty packs in the last two weeks alone."

"You're counting my gum wads?" I felt my eyes narrow. I didn't make them do it; they sort of went all squinty on their own. "That doesn't strike you as, oh, I dunno, anal-retentive?"

"Doesn't your depositing them all over the house," she snapped back, annoyingly unafraid, "strike you as incredibly selfish and slovenly?"

"For the lasht time, thish ish none of your bithneth."

What the—? Horrified, I felt my mouth.

Marc was pointing at me, eyes big. "Your fangs are out! You got so pissed your fangs came out!"

"I thought they only came out when you smelled blood," Jessica said, still remarkably unmoved.

"They do," I replied, feeling. Cripes, it felt like I had a mouthful of needles. "But Sinclair can make his come out whenever he wanth. Maybe thith ith part of a new power."

"And maybe you're, I dunno, *losing it*!"

"Calm down. Thereth nothing to worry about."

"Nothing to worry about?" Marc was as hysterical as a woman who missed all the really good Thanksgiving sales. "You should see yourself!"

"Well, maybe I'll go take a walk." Oh, and run into that cute Mrs. Lentz in her bouncy, thin-strapped jogging bra while she walks her border collie. Normally I went for guys but her shoulders were so lovely and bare—

"You can't go out looking like *that*."

I was hurt. Well, pretending to be. "Are you thaying I thould be athamed? Thith is who I am now."

"Yes," Marc said, and Jessica swallowed her laugh. "You should be very, very ashamed. You should go to your room and hide your head until the shame passes. And until you don't look like you're trying out for the next *Dracula* remake."

A sly thought popped into my head, there and gone, one

Eric would understand, and so would Alonzo

too slippery to hold on to. Probably just as well. These days, none of my thoughts were nice ones.

"Doeth anybody have thum gum? I'm freth out."

"Sure," Jessica said brightly, as if a wonderful idea had just occurred to her, "and hey, maybe this time you can stick the wads in a garbage can, if you want to avoid eviction." She slid a brand-new pack of strawberry Bubblicious toward me.

"I'll second that motion," Marc mumbled. "Honestly, Betsy, do you know what they *put* in that stuff? The artificial gunk that slides down your throat, leaving the hard, gray crud behind?"

"Thut up," I told him, reaching for the pack. "Thith ithn't very conthructive."

"Yeah? Constructive is the last damned thing on my mind. This place drives me nuts sometimes: nutty vampires, a bitchy werewolf, a zombie, a grumpy billionaire, and a vampire on a hunger strike."

"You have to admit," Jessica said, starting to put away the liquor bottles, "there's never a dull moment. What's the polar opposite of a dull moment? 'Cuz that's what we got around here. All the time."

"I don't think you should call Garrett a zombie. He's a little slow, but—hey! Don't take the vodka."

"You can have it back," she said in her annoying Mommy voice, "when your fangs go away."

"I can have it back right *now,* honey."

Marc put his hands over his eyes. "Don't fight, you guys. No more. I'm sincere here."

She slapped my hand when I reached for it. "No! Bad vampire!"

I glared. "You know, most sensible people would be scared of me."

She laughed at me. "Most sensible people haven't seen you dancing the Pancake Dance in your granny underpants on New Year's Eve."

"Hey! Your fangs are gone." Marc digested what she'd just said. "Granny underpants? You?" Apparently me doing the Pancake Dance wasn't so hard to believe.

"It was just that one time," I grumbled, the last of my mad-on vanishing as quickly as it had come upon me. "All my thongs were in the wash." What had I even been so mad about, anyway? I couldn't remember. Jessica and Marc were the greatest. I was lucky to have friends like them. They were—

The kitchen door swung open, framing the former head of the Blood Warriors. "I don't understand," Jon Delk said. "You're saying I published a book?"

—sunk. We all were.

CHAPTER 19

"Thanks for coming so quickly."

Delk hadn't taken off his coat, and had tracked mud all the way (groan) to the kitchen. His full name was Jonathon Michael Delk, but too many people in his life called him Jonny. So he was going all tough guy now and insisting on the moniker Delk. I couldn't blame him: I had a silly first name, too.

"She said you were in trouble," J—er, Delk was saying. "But it sounds like that was just another vampire trick to get me to—"

"I said the Queen needed you," Tina corrected him with more than a little sharpness. Tina didn't care for Delk, given his vampire-slaying past. No doubt the car ride up from the farm had been a carnival. Not least because she and Eric thought it was perfectly fine to leave Jon out of it. But I just couldn't do it. He had written the book. It was being published. How could I keep my mouth shut about it?

"Delk, sit down."

"What's going on?" He shook the catalog at me, dropped it

on the table, and rubbed his hands together; they were red with cold. "One minute I'm home, the next I'm in the car with Tina—"

"Do you want something to warm up with?"

He gave me a look I supposed he thought was subtle. I was feeling sicker and sicker by the moment, and it wasn't all the failed rainbows. Delk had a bit of a crush on me, and if he had come charging up to the Cities because he thought I was in trouble—well, that was just too damned sweet.

In fact, he'd shown up here a few months ago when he heard about my impending unholy nuptials. The gist of our conversation:

> DELK: You can't marry Eric Sinclair.
> ME: Just watch.
> DELK: He's a bad man.
> ME: You don't know from bad.
> DELK: You're making a mistake.
> ME: Shut your head.

Not exactly Tristan and Isolde, but it passed the time around here.

Then, inexplicably (except I was pretty sure I knew why) he hung around the mansion. Started interviewing me for a class project. Eventually produced a book. But then Sinclair—

"Tina, would you leave us alone for a minute?"

"I'll go see if the king is available," she said, backing out of the kitchen, looking at Delk the way a cat looked at a really big rat. *I can take you. I might get hurt, but that's all right.*

We were alone. Except for Marc and Jessica, shamelessly eavesdropping outside the kitchen door. I couldn't do anything about that, so I addressed the problem at hand. "You wrote the book. It's coming out this fall as a paperback everyone thinks is funny fiction."

"You're saying someone used my name on their book?"

Oh, boy. He was standing there, so earnest and flushed and blond and *young,* I almost couldn't bear it. He was a nice kid. I liked him a lot. There never would have been anything between us, and not just because of Sinclair, but I still liked him and sure didn't want to upset him.

I could almost hear Sinclair in my head: *Then don't.*

Too bad.

"I'm saying you wrote this book, this *Undead and Unwed.* Someone—probably you—turned it into a publisher, and now it's going to be on bookshelves this fall."

"But—I mean, I did a paper for class before holiday break—"

"You turned the paper into a book. You followed me around for days, transcribing my life story, putting your own spin on it. You had, like, three hundred pages."

He was blinking so fast, for a second I thought he had something in both eyes. "But I don't remember that! I'd remember if I wrote a book, right?"

"Yeah, normally. Except Sinclair made you forgot you'd written it. And since you didn't remember writing it, you didn't think to warn us that you'd sent it in to get published."

"*Warn* you? I—" He walked dazedly back and forth by the table for a moment, not quite pacing. He looked like he didn't know what to do with his hands. "Sinclair made me forget?"

"Well." Tell the truth and shame my sister's mother, wasn't that how the saying went? Sure, we could be done now, but I didn't want any part of this conversation left undead. Whoops— Freudian slip. *Unsaid.* Another surprise down the road I didn't

need. "Tina found the electronic version of your manuscript—
she was looking for it, or something like it—and told Sinclair.
He mojoed you into forgetting all about it, and then they
deleted your work. They thought all of your work."

"Did you call me down here," he whispered, "because you
just found out and you want my help to stop them?"

"Ah, no. See, after they did all that, they told me. This was
around Christmas. And at first I told Sinclair to undo his
undoing, if you get what I mean. But then I remembered."

"What?"

"I remembered I'm the queen and I'm responsible for all
the vampires," I said simply. "So I let it all stand. It was shitty
for you, but I thought if the book got out that would be shitty
for all vampires."

He was clutching the back of one of the kitchen chairs and
I saw all the knuckles had gone from pink to dead white. All
the color had fallen out of his face, except for two patches of
red way up on each cheek.

"Are you okay?" I asked, dumbest question of the year, no
doubt. "Maybe you better sit down."

"You—you *let*—him—*do* that? To me?"

"Well, I didn't know about it until afterward," I began lamely,
"but—"

He actually swayed a little while he hung onto the chair. I
edged a little closer, figuring I could catch him if he fainted.
He *looked* like he was going to faint. After he threw up. "You
let him do that—let him into my fucking *mind*—and then you
had the chance to *help* me and you took *their* side?"

"I—yeah. That's more or less it."

"You didn't help me—you let him—and you didn't—"

"Delk, I think you should sit down before you—"

"Shut! Up!" he screamed at me, the cords standing out on his neck. "You aren't *even* sorry! Because if you did it, if you fucked me over to help all of goddamn vampire-kind, you *can't* be sorry."

"I'm sorry you got stuck in the middle. I'm sorry there's a book out there that you don't remember writing. A funny book the critics like," I added, trying to find a speckle of good in this whole awful nightmare. Oooh, and there was something else! "You kind of got the last laugh, because the book is coming out anyway, and the vampires who know about it are pretty annoyed, so—"

"So everything you let him *do* to me was for nothing."

"Okay, that's another way to look at it."

He wiped his nose with the back of the hand not holding the chair. "I can't believe this," he whispered.

"I'm really sor—"

"I can believe that bitch snuck around in my files, and I can believe that prick jumped into my mind, but you! You're supposed to be the good one! I-I thought you—you aren't supposed to be a bad guy! You're supposed to look out for me, *and* for vampires—they're all the same to you, right?"

I stammered, trying to say five things at once.

"Right?"

"Delk, I—"

He wheeled around and almost slipped in one of the little puddles he'd made.

"Please don't leave! Please, let's talk some more."

He barked an incredulous laugh, staggered for the door and shoved against it, hard.

Unfortunately, it only moved about a foot before it thudded into something.

"Aagghh!" I heard Jessica say from the other side, then another thud as she fell down. I rushed over, held the door open, and saw her rolling back and forth on the floor, hands cupped around her nose. The blood, it was—it was *sheeting* down her throat and onto her shirt; the blouse was already wrecked.

Marc was crouched beside her, doing the doctor/mom chant: "No, I won't touch it, just let me look, no, I'm not going to touch, just get your hands down so I can see, let me see."

That was no ordinary nosebleed. It was just—it was everywhere. I whirled upon Delk. "She's sick! And you practically broke her nose—she didn't do *anything*. And she's *sick,* you asshole!"

Before I knew what was happening, I had seized him by the shirt and was holding him right up to my nose. "You thouhd have kept your handth to yourthelf."

"Betsy, don't! It was an accident, come on, it's—" Jessica choked a little from her spot on the floor and spat blood. "It's a swinging door, for heaven's sake. I'm surprised this doesn't happen every week. Come on, put him down."

I threw him away from me. He bounced off the wall (and I'd be lying if I didn't admit it felt good to watch him fly like a paper airplane, and where had all my sympathy for him gone?) and crumpled to the floor in a heap.

I knelt by my friends. "Jeth, are you all ri—"

"Look out!" she screamed, and I turned just in time to get shot.

I'll bet Marc is sorry he skipped work today, I thought, toppling into Jessica's bloody face and knocking her down again.

CHAPTER 20

I woke up just in time to hear Jon's bellow of pain and the instantaneous dull "snap" that came with it.

Get up

I tried to move.

Get up or they'll kill each other. Really kill each other.

My entire chest felt like it had been drenched in kerosene and then lit. And not in a good way, either. I tried to sit up.

"Better not," Marc said, and I realized he and Jessica were both kneeling over me. "I think your heart's busy growing back."

"Help me up," I groaned.

"Bad idea," he said, but he carefully pulled me to my feet. It seemed to take a long time.

"Jess, you okay?"

"I'm fine. Nothing's broken." She looked awful—blood all over her clothes, blood drying across her face—but at least it wasn't fresh blood. "I know this isn't the time or place, but that really squicks me out."

"What?"

"You're licking blood off the back of your hand," Marc murmured.

Yeesh! "Sorry." I made myself stop. Just as well; it hurt to move. Luckily I didn't need to breathe, because I bet that would have hurt like crazy, too. Now where was I? Something important. Like, life or death important. Oh, yeah . . . "Stop, you guys! Cut it out. Sinclair, let him go."

Not that I could see what was going on, but it wasn't hard to guess.

I limped toward the kitchen door (which had started all the trouble, come to think of it) and pushed it open. Sinclair was just leaning down to pick Jon up off the tiles, ignoring the loaded gun pointed at his nose.

"Ah, you're up and around," Sinclair said, looking over at me. "Splendid."

"Just . . . stop. Okay? Come on. I got shot, you broke Delk's arm, Jess got a nosebleed. We'll sprain Marc's ankle and make Tina have a haircut and then everybody's even, okay? Please don't," I pleaded, as Sinclair reached for his prey again. "It's so awful right now; please let's not make it worse. Besides, aren't you dying to rush over here and make sure for yourself that I'm all right?"

I could see him think about it. The gun might have been made of candy for all he noticed it, but I knew Jon's bullets were hollow points stuffed with holy water. One probably would have killed Sinclair. As usual (happy sigh), when I was concerned, he didn't give much of a shit about his personal safety.

And yup, he was actually wrestling with his lovely desire to check on me. And his strong male urge to pull Delk's head off his shoulders and use it as a soccer ball.

"Please," I said again, and abruptly Sinclair straightened up, leaving the other man flat on his back and waving his gun at nothing. He crossed the room and grabbed my hands, then held them out so he could stare at my chest. Marc had ripped my shirt open while I was out; luckily, it was a bra day. I looked down; no hole. Just a few trickles of dried blood.

"*Are* you right?"

My Ipex bra would never be the same, but . . . "Sore as hell."

He shook his head. "You are miraculous. The bullet should have killed you. At the least, you should not be healing so quickly, especially as you haven't had any blood in—four days?"

I made a face. "Don't remind me."

He kissed me. "I am thankful for all your peculiarities." He said it with a fervor that made me smile, but a cold part of me wondered what Delk must think of all this cooing vampire affection. Not much, I imagined.

"I'll see the boy out," Tina offered. She'd come in, unnoticed as usual, and was standing by the back stairs. "The boy," heh. No more of "your friend" or "the young gentleman" or "Jon" or even "Mr. Delk" Nope, the gloves were off.

"No, you won't," I wheezed, because she looked positively drooley at the thought of getting Jon alone for a moment. "I'll see him out." I was pretty sure I could make the walk from here to the front door without falling down.

Pretty sure.

"Well, *I'm* not going to," Jessica said. "Marc, you help her."

"I've got patients here."

At some point, Jon had climbed to his feet. The gun was still out, was swinging wildly as he tried to point at all of us at once. His other arm was bent at a nauseating angle; I wondered how he was able to get to his feet, never mind stand

and keep the gun up. His face had gone the color of oatmeal. Sweat was standing out on his forehead in big drops. "Nobody sees me out! None of you *freaks* come near me. I'll see myself out."

"Well, all right, don't make a big thing of it," I said crossly. "You know, I *should* be yelling at you for shooting me, but I'm going to let the whole thing go. Now we're even for everything, right?"

"Fuck you," he replied, sounding cool and tough, and we all pretended not to see the tears rimming his lower lashes. "You're only alive because I—because I didn't want you dead just yet."

"Whatever sustains your fragile young male ego. But I think you'd be better off coming back here with an improved attitude."

"You'll see me again," he promised. "With attitude and more." Then he let the gun sort of drift to his side—it was probably way too painful to put it, one-handed, back into a shoulder holster—and simply walked away. On his way through the foyer, he steadied himself once on the banister— and drew his hand away in disgust, shaking stale gum off his fingers.

"And you wanted to evict me," I gently chided Jessica.

Delk stumbled up against the giant front doors, wrestled with the nineteenth-century knob, swore at the latch, got the door open, swore some more at us . . . and was gone.

"He's got a lot of personal growth ahead of him," I observed. My chest felt a lot better; had the bullet gone through me? It must have. I hoped so; I didn't want Marc or anyone else digging around in there to find it again.

"The infant is lucky he choose to leave."

"We did some pretty shitty things to the infant, in case you forgot. Or don't you care about that?"

Sinclair was eyeing the ruins of my ripped shirt, the bloodstains. "No," he said flatly. "I don't care about that."

CHAPTER 21

"We can't let him live," Tina said.

"Sure we can."

"Majesty, be reasonable. I know you are—were—fond of the child, but he is a *dangerous* child."

"I still consider him a friend, okay? Friends have fallings-outs. Or would that be fallings-out? Anyway, we don't always get along a hundred percent of the time. Look at me and Jessica!"

"Duh *not*," Little Miss Myeloma said, her voice muffled through the ice pak Marc had slapped over her face, "drag meh entoh this."

We were in the (first) parlor. We'd picked it because there were two couches, and Jessica and I both needed one. Shit, I needed a hospital ward. But a couch that smelled like dust was the best I could do, right now.

"Surely after what happened today you do not still consider him an ally?"

"Eric, try to see his point of view! If someone's keeping

score, we're ahead of him on points, okay? So, seriously: don't go after him, you guys. Don't order another vampire to do it, either. Jon's out of bounds as far as the vampires are concerned."

"Foolish sentimentality."

"Hey, I'm mad at him, too, okay? He shot me. In the chest. With holy water. But I'm not going to kill him."

Everybody looked at my chest.

"No, seriously. He didn't mean to do that. Or he meant to, but he knew it wouldn't kill me—he was scared, okay? Scared and humiliated, which is just the worst combo ever. At least the worst part's over."

"Worst part?" Jessica mumbled around her ice pack.

"I was really dreading telling him. I did *not* want to do that, boy oh boy. But at least it's out."

"What I'd like to know," Marc said from his chair by the fire, "is what he was doing here with a gun in the first place."

"Are you kidding? That kid's always got about nine guns and knives on him. Those farm boys are tough."

"Right," Marc allowed, "but a former Blood Warrior shows up, and you guys don't even frisk him? Make him walk through a metal detector? Something?"

"We knew he was carrying. Mostly because he's *always* carrying. But we never frisk anybody."

"What, that's a rule now?"

"Sure," I said, and Sinclair nodded, backing me up.

"Come on, guys! The Queen of England's a tough cookie, too; but she puts people through a metal detector and a security check before they can talk to her."

"If the throne is so easily taken from us," Sinclair explained, almost exactly the way he explained it to me, "we would be poor monarchs indeed."

"In other words, if someone gets the drop on you in your own house, too bad for Betsy and Sinclair, but they should have been able to take care of themselves?"

We looked at each other. "Basically," I answered, "yeah."

"Great," Marc muttered, and slumped lower in his chair. "Those of us caught in the crossfire appreciate the attention to detail."

"Although," I said, looking at Jessica's face—what I could see around the ice, "maybe we should change that rule."

"If we cannot protect our allies," Sinclair said, "the same rule applies."

"Tough luck, guys," I said in a fake-bright laugh, and they both laughed.

"Getting back to the issue of the child," Tina said, harshing our buzz as usual, "I really think you should reconsider. He—"

The phone rang. She picked it up, glanced at the caller ID.

"We're kind of busy," I said, a little sharply. The phone was a whole thing between Tina and me.

"But—"

"If it's important, they'll call back."

"But it's your mother."

I practically snarled. The phone, the fucking phone! People used it the way they used to use the cat-o'-nine-tails. You had to drop everything and answer the fucking thing. And God help you if you were home and, for whatever reason, didn't answer. "But I called!" Yeah, it was convenient for *you* so you called. But I'm in the shit because it wasn't convenient for *me* to drop everything and talk to *you,* on the spot, for whatever *you* needed to talk about.

Unfortunately, Tina was the type who lunged for it every time it so much as peeped. She couldn't stand the sound of a ringing phone. Always tracked me down: it's so-and-so. Well, I'm *recovering from a fatal chest wound, take a message*. But it's your mother! Yeah, well, she'll call back. But she's on the phone *now*.

I practically snatched it from her. "Hi, Mom, this really isn't a good t—"

"Your grandfather," Mom said in the doleful voice reserved for announcing funerals, "has escaped."

"Escaped what? Mom? He's got three kinds of cancer, he's eighty-nine, and he's hooked up to forty different machines. What are you talking about, escaped?"

"Someone's coming up the driveway," Tina said in a low voice.

"Well, go take care of it."

"And if they need to see you, Majesty?"

I cupped a hand over the mouthpiece. "Read my royal lips, Tina: *this is not a good time*."

"What?" my mom said.

"I wasn't talking to you, Mom. See, the reason I sound all distracted right now is because *this is not a good time*."

"Well, why did you answer the phone then?" my mom asked reasonably. "Just let it ring."

"*Gah!* Tell me about Grandpa, please."

"Well, you know he doesn't care for that nursing home."

"Right. So what else is new. The guy's got three kinds of cancer. And frankly, it probably isn't much fun for the nursing home to have him there."

"This is true," Mom replied promptly. She had, after all, been raised by the gentleman in question. "Anyway, he doesn't like it there. The animals are the least of it."

I had to laugh. The animals! Apparently all these studies

had been done about how soothing and restful nursing home inmates—uh, residents—found live-in cats, dogs, and birds.

So my grandpa's nursing home adopted all these strays, and told incoming residents, *why, of course you can keep your angry, incontinent, biting dog Nibbles! No problemo! Bring all his brothers and sisters, too! Share them with the other residents!*

On paper, this is a swell idea. What the genius who did the study didn't take into account was: Grandpa Joe. Maybe he had only nice, soft-spoken old ladies and gentlemen in the study.

Grandpa had grown up on a farm, and had a very pragmatic view of animals: *if I can't eventually kill you and eat you, you are taking up valuable air and space.* My mom never had a pet—not so much as a goldfish in a bowl—the entire time she was growing up. Neither had I, until I'd moved out after college and picked up Giselle the cat from the pound.

The animals had pretty much taken over the nursing home. They had the run of the place, and took ruthless advantage of it. And they certainly made the staff feel better. *Ohhh, how cute, that cat is helping that man with all the terminal illnesses!*

So now, my grandfather, who should be enjoying his autumn years, has to boot a snoozing golden retriever out of his bed if he wants to snag a nap after lunch.

"Well, he just couldn't take it anymore," Mom was saying. "So he unhooked all the equipment he was on—"

"Um, hello, didn't any alarms go off in the nursing station?"

"Well, hon, you know how understaffed they are. And Grandpa lulled them into a false sense of security by pulling his leads out a bunch of other times."

"Like the boy who cried wolf," I suggested. The angry

cancer-raddled animal-hater who cried wolf, repeatedly, to fool his captors. I mean the nurses. "Except a whole bunch of times."

"Right. So nobody thought much of it when the alarms went off—they figured Joe was up to his old tricks again. So he got into his chair—"

"He can transfer by himself now?" I knew all the lingo from a brief, but memorable, stint as a volunteer at that very home.

"Yes. So he got into his wheelchair and—you know. Escaped."

"Just wheeled himself out past the border guard, huh?"

"Exactly. You know—oh, look, that sweet old man is coming out to see the world."

"Morons," I decided.

"Yes, but they couldn't know. They aren't family. Anyway, out he goes—"

"Out*side*?"

"I know, I know."

"It's twenty fucking degrees outside!"

"Well, more like ten there." There being Brainerd, Minnesota. "But sadly, your grandfather did not foresee see his old enemy, fatigue, when he made his daring dash for freedom."

"Where did he think he was going to go in a hospital johnny?" I wondered. Dumb question. For Grandpa, being half-naked was irrelevant. Being master of your own destiny was all! "How far did he get?"

"About three blocks outside the home and then fell asleep. A family on the way to visit a relative ratted him out."

"Vile informers!" I cried.

"So the nurses came to get him, and wheeled him back, and tucked him back into bed—he was so exhausted he didn't even wake up—and imagine how completely irritated he was when he woke up with a cat on his pillow!"

I shuddered, imagining Grandpa's wrath. As a member of The Greatest Generation, he wasn't adverse to blowing shit up to get his way.

"The important thing is, he's okay."

"Betsy, what am I going to do? He hates it there. I mean he *hates* it. How can I keep my own father in a place that he hates?"

"You could revel in the payback for a horrible childhood?" I guessed.

"Elizabeth." On this, as in very few other things, my mom had no sense of humor. I guess when you spent your childhood dodging fists and trying not to get kicked down stairs, it wasn't much fun to joke about it later. "You're not helping."

"Come on, Mom, it's a nursing home. He's lucky he's not in a hospital. Actually, he's lucky he's not dead."

"That's true," she said doubtfully.

"Although, if he's peppy enough to escape, he maybe could be moved some other place."

"Maybe. But where? Any place private is too expensive."

"Yeah." I looked over at Marc, who was tenderly touching Jessica's nose and murmuring to her. She in turn had just finished telling him a heartwarming Grandpa Joe story she had previously heard from me, probably the one involving grenades and the minister. "Listen, I've got an idea about that. My roommate, Marc, has a—"

"Oh, that clever doctor. Did I tell you I met the perfect man for him? He's a grad student, getting his doctorate in Japanese literature—"

"Yeah, that sounds really fun and useful. Listen, his father has this place—they must have some like it up where Joe is, but if not, maybe we could move him down here . . ."

"What kind of place?"

I told her. And that was how I ended up with my Grandpa Joe living four miles away from my vampire-infested house. Which may or may not, now that I look back, have been a greater hazard to my health than having my heart temporarily blown up by holy water.

I never did find out who had popped in for a surprise visit. Which was fine with me. More surprises, I so did not need.

CHAPTER 22

"You realize of course that, once he gets transferred down here, you'll have to visit him. When he was a four-hour drive away, that was one thing, but now you could walk there in ten minutes."

"Shut up," I moaned, "shut up, shut *up*."

"I have to admit," Jessica went on cheerfully—why wouldn't she be cheerful, the swelling had gone down and *her* grandparents were dead. "I'm amazed he's still alive. Didn't they tell you *last* year that he had only months to live?"

"Three months," I remembered. "They gave him three months."

"Wow. And now here he's going to be living with Marc's father!"

"Yes, it's all a rich tapestry of horror and survival. Where's a perfectly made rainbow drink when you need one?"

"Marc's sleeping," she said, "and you can't blame him. Guy finally gets a day off, and spends it taking care of his room-mates."

"Finally, having a doctor in the house pays off."

"I know I'm feeling better—how about you?"

"Fine." Which was true. When I'd risen that afternoon, it was like nothing happened. If not for the ruined T-shirt and sports bra in the garbage, I'd guess nothing had happened.

Sinclair had seen for himself, pulling off my bra the minute our bedroom door had closed, going over my chest and back inch by inch. Which had turned into him going over my crotch inch by inch. Repeat as needed. The evening had turned out so terrific, it made it almost—

No, I didn't mean that. It wasn't worth it no matter how much sex I'd had. I didn't mind getting shot nearly as much as I minded Jessica and Delk getting hurt.

And oh, boy, the look on Delk's face in the kitchen as everything dawned on him. That was one I'd take to my grave. Assuming I ever went there for any other reason than to visit the currently premature tombstone.

"Delk will be back," Jessica said, trying to cheer me up.

"Yeah, I know. That's what I'm worried about."

The phone rang, and I gave the wall extension an ugly look. It rang again. Jessica got up and said, "I know, you're not here. It might be about your grandpa's transfer . . . hello?"

I stirred my tea, and simmered next to it. Like Korben Dallas in *The Fifth Element,* I was sure all communications were ultimately bad news. Why hasten it by cutting out the middle man?

"Uh-huh," Jessica was saying. "I'm not sure that's—uh-huh . . . yeah . . . yeah, but—listen, I'm just not sure if—let me just ask her, okay? She's right—hello?"

Jessica hung up and looked at me.

"Hours later or a day late?"

"Your stepmother won't be able to get the baby for another

couple of hours." Jessica looked at the clock on the wall. "It's still early. I guess she—uh—lost track of—look, this doesn't prove your stupid telephone theory, okay?"

I could hear BabyJon's fretful squealing getting closer and closer. Then the kitchen door opened and Sinclair poked his head in. "The baby wants you," he called, and the door swung shut. Then I saw the door open again as Sinclair held the port-a-crib in his arms. It was a little too wide, fully open and extended, to go through the door, so Sinclair squished it a little and it popped through.

I leapt to my feet as Jessica cracked up. "You carried the whole crib down here? Stop that, you're *folding* him up in it!"

"He has plenty of room on all sides," Sinclair said, louder, to be heard over BabyJon's escalating wails.

"Just pick him up! Or leave him there and come and get me, jeez." I picked him up and he quieted. "Don't blame you for that one, yes, Uncle Sinclair is a big poopie-head, isn't he?"

"I am not his uncle," he replied, making a beeline for the liquor cabinet, "and if I was, it would be Uncle Eric."

"It's Uncle Schmuck right now, bud! I can't believe you just dragged the whole thing down here, all unfolded and everything . . ."

"He seems fine," Sinclair said, dumping a shot of brandy into an empty teacup, which he then filled with hot water from the kettle.

"We're out of English Breakfast, so ha."

"I will struggle along." He gave the baby a look. "You are expecting your stepmother presently, yes?"

"She's running late."

"Hours late or a day late?"

How well they were coming to know The Ant! It was enough to make me want to cry. No, that was the smell BabyJon's diaper was giving off. "Hours," I said, nearly choking.

"I think that kid does have supernatural powers," Jessica observed as I gagged and looked around wildly for the diaper bag. "Powers in his pants."

"You guys. He's just a baby, doing what all babies do." I could hear the resonant chime of our front door bell. "Maybe that's the Ant!"

Sinclair called something out to me, but I didn't hear it. Okay, wasn't listening. Anyway, I practically galloped through the rooms and the halls that led to the front door. All would be forgiven if I could get out of changing this one sinister diaper.

I swung open the door.

"Majesty," the strange but familiar vampire said. She had a calm center that resembled Alonzo's. Had she been with the European delegation? Yes, I believed she had. Her small stature and close-cropped carroty red hair jogged my memory along. "I beg your indulgence in coming by without an appointment."

"Uh." I shifted BabyJon to my other arm. "That's okay. Uh—"

"Carolina."

"Right. Carolina. What's up."

"I was just—" She looked around on the front step.

"Oh! Sorry, come in."

"Thank you, Majesty." She followed me in and swung the big door shut. "I will not keep you long. I was only wondering if you had decided Alonzo's fate." She seemed perfectly calm, but she couldn't have been. Unless she saw me as no threat whatsoever, and decided to swing by the mansion on the way to Caribou Coffee.

"You were? Wondering, I mean?"

"Yes, ma'am. We all are. Alonzo most of all, of course, but he has surprisingly little to say about you, which is frustrating for the rest of us, as you can imagine." She gave me a small, hopeful smile as if to say, *isn't all this just so silly?*

"Well, it's nice of you to check in."

She shrugged. "He is my cousin."

"Oh! I didn't know that."

She looked puzzled, and rubbed her nose for a moment. Then rubbed it again. Maybe she was trying to get rid of the freckles. "We were introduced."

"Right, right. Well, about that—I'm sorry you guys are sort of stuck there waiting—you don't have to—" I realized what I was saying and stopped. Of course, they had to. She in particular, if they were family. Family! Real honest to God family; here I'd thought I was the only vampire with blood relatives. And what were the others supposed to do while this little Sophie/Alonzo/Liam triangle was resolved? Blow town and leave their buddy to swing?

But they couldn't exactly go around doing their normal vampire things while this was hanging over their head. And they had to be wondering if they were all going to be painted with the same brush when, and if, Alonzo was punished. Trouble was . . . "I didn't mean to leave you guys all waiting."

"Majesty, it is too bold of me to come by and ask your intentions, but it would not be the first time my curiosity led me down a sorry path."

"Yeah, sorry about that."

"Do you smell something horrible?" she asked, looking at my brother.

"Yeah, well, he's had a lot of bottles today—"

"That is your *brother*?"

"Yeah. Look, that's a whole other—"

"I thought you only had a sister."

"Right, the devil's daughter, but—"

"But how interesting! You must tell me more."

BabyJon blatted and I felt his diaper get warmer. And heavier. *No! Hull integrity would not hold! She's losing it, Captain, she's losing it!*

"Carolina!"

She jumped, and I continued before she could react further. "Look, I'm sorry, but I just can't talk to you right now. Everything's just a mess: my best friend's horribly sick and my other friend's got a crush on Alonzo, I'm stuck babysitting hours past what I agreed to, this kid is shitting up every diaper he gets near, one of my subjects wants to turn her human boyfriend, my birthday's at the end of the week and I'm off blood, my grandpa's sick and he's moving in just down the street, I got shot in the chest with holy water by a young farm boy with a crush on me, and my life story is the promising new fall book. On top of that, I haven't done a fucking thing to prepare for my wedding in three months. It is—how do you say this in Europe?—just *not a fucking good time right now*."

Carolina had backed up until her back was flat against the door. "So sorry to intrude," she said.

I took a step forward, fragile baby-and-poop bomb bouncing tenderly in my arms. My mouth was beginning to hurt. "Sometimes, I just feel like I'm going to break, you know what I mean? Can you imagine?"

"Yes, Majesty."

"Really, you can? Because I figure it's gotta be something

pretty fucking spectacular when a Vampire Queen lights up. I mean, just goes off the deep end. Lets the blood boil and the teeth fly. Have you ever acthually theen that happen?"

"I cannot say that I have, Your Majesty."

My tongue played around the sharp edges of my teeth. Her scent was fascinating—she had turned when young, and even the passage of centuries of evil deeds could not cloud a certain divine innocence. "Would you like to? You and I can lock ourthelves in a thpare room, and I can focuth on your particular thituation and conthernth, and we can thee who leaves the room a few hourth later. Hmm?"

"I will go now. See? I am making no sudden moves." She slowly turned and reached for the doorknob. She was far more facile with the nineteenth-century technology than Delk had been; she was immediately back in the safety of open air. "Good . . . evening . . . Majesty . . ."

The door clicked closed.

"I think," Sinclair's smooth voice came from behind me, "You are finally getting the hang of this, my love."

As my fangs slowly receded, I didn't know whether to thank him or throw the baby-bomb at him.

CHAPTER 23

"Laura, I'm so sorry to do this to you again."

"Betsy, it's fine. I'm delighted to help out." She nuzzled the baby. "And delighted ooo see ooo again! Is ooo my best wittle boy? Is ooo?"

"Really, really sorry. But I had plans for tonight and frankly, if I don't do this now, I'll never psych myself up to do it again."

She had all the baby crap, was hauling it (and BabyJon) easily into the front hall. "Betsy, will you stop? It's my pleasure to help out. You'll let his mom know?"

"Yeah, well, she's not gonna be happy when she finds out I shirked BabyJon on you. Just remind her not to shoot the messenger."

Laura laughed, shaking her blonde hair away from her face. "Goodness! I'm sure she'll be fine. You know, Betsy, Mrs. Taylor isn't nearly as bad as you—"

Okay, if I had to get the "give your stepmother a chance" lecture from someone who hadn't grown up with her, I was going to pop a blood vessel. "Yeah, well, thanks, I owe you, bye!" I gave her a helpful shove.

I closed the big front door and leaned on it. Right. BabyJon given the bootie: check. Sinclair off with Tina somewhere: check. No pop-ins that I knew of: check. Marc at work: check. Toni and Garrett prowling around outside, him to eat and her for kicks: check (I made a mental note to make sure those two were only fucking with bad guys). Cathie-the-ghost nowhere in evidence: check.

Jessica knitting in her room: check.

She had a largish room on the second floor, the one with the blue and gold wallpaper and all the trim and old furniture in blond wood, as if the Scandinavian carpenters who built this mansion so long ago were thinking of their wives' hair when they designed and built it.

I rapped on the half-closed door and went in at her, "C'mon in."

Knitting in bed was a new thing. Usually she brought her yarn bag into the kitchen with us, or went into the basement with Garrett, or took it to a craft class. But Marc had explained that she got tired earlier, and took longer to get going when she got up.

"Got a minute?" I asked.

"Uh-huh."

"I can't tell where the one on the bed is, and the one you're working on starts," I joked. It was true, though: she was lying on a navy crocheted coverlet, and crocheting another one, this one red.

"Yeah, well, you're an idiot." She grinned.

"Uh-huh." I barely heard the insult. I started to sit on the bed, then got up and sort of prowled around the foot of it for a moment. "Listen, Jess, I've been doing a lot of thinking lately. I mean, a *lot*."

"Do you need some Advil?"

"This is serious!" I almost shouted at her. "Listen—I can't believe I'm even talking to you about this—"

"No," she said.

"What?"

"No. You can't bite me. You can't turn me into a vampire. I won't allow it."

My oft-rehearsed speech disappeared in a whirl of relief and indignation. "What? How did you know? Oh, those big-mouthed idiots!"

"Yes, that's how I'd describe Tina and Sinclair. Come on, Betsy. Nobody had to tell me. It was so obvious—not only are you having private conversations with experienced vampires, but frankly, every time you look at me it's like a dog looking at a raw steak."

"Huh."

"Yeah."

"Listen, I'm sorry about the looks, but I've done some research, and the risks—"

"Are a lot higher if you bite me, than if I treat my cancer."

I opened my mouth.

"Because pretty it up how you want, you're still killing me, right?"

I closed my mouth and she went on, in a nice but totally firm way. "Even if I come back after. And if I *do* come back after, there's no guarantee I'll be me, right? In fact, it sounds like for at least the first few years, I'll be a mindless blood-sucking automaton. No thank you."

"Anything sounds bad when you put 'mindless' and 'sucking'

in front of it." I flopped down on the end of her bed. "Jeez, days I've been working up to this, grilling everybody, screwing up the courage to talk to you about it, and you're all, 'yeah, I knew what you were going to say, and by the way, no.'"

"It's not my fault it's pathetically easy to read your minuscule mind."

I gave her a look. "I guess this is the part where I'm all 'you *will* be mine, O yes' and you're all 'eeeek, unhand me, I'd rather die than join in your unholy crusade.'"

"No, that was last winter when you wanted me to go Christmas shopping in early October."

"Christmas shopping in October is just efficient."

"Trust you," she sneered, "to get *grotesque* and *efficient* mixed up."

"Why do I want to save you and keep you around for eternity again?"

She shrugged. "Beats me."

I looked at the ceiling, because I didn't want to look at her. I didn't want to try to figure out if her color was off, if she'd lost weight. "Jessica, this thing might kill you."

"So your response is . . . to kill me?"

"It's a chance for some kind of life. A life where your best friend is the queen. That's got to be worth something."

She nudged my shoulder with a toe. "You're glossing over all the things that could go wrong."

"Well, so are you!"

"There's time. Time to fight this. I'm sorry—I can see it's been a little on the agonizing side for you. But typical Betsy—you assumed this was something *you* had to decide. It's my life, and my death, and I'm choosing to stand and fight." She smiled. "Besides, if you turn me into a vampire, I don't think we can hide that from Nick. And then he'll know for sure!"

"The least of my problems," I said glumly. Then I said, "You haven't told him yet?"

"I'm saving it," she said, suddenly glum, too, "for our two-month-aversary."

What a phenomenally bad idea. Also, none of my business. "If that's how you feel . . ."

"That's entirely, exactly how I feel. So no sneaking around and leaping out at me from the shadows to try and turn me, okay?" She picked up her afghan, and got back to work.

Good example for all of us.

"Okay," I said, getting up and walking toward the door, "but if you change your mind and decide you want to be foully murdered—"

"I'll run up to your room first thing," she promised.

Mollified, I left.

CHAPTER 24

I didn't get far.

"Hey," Cathie said, walking through the wall at the top of the stairs.

"Hey."

"I wasn't eavesdropping," she began defensively.

I groaned.

"Well, I wasn't. I was coming to get you."

"Why?"

She shrugged. "No ghosts around to talk to right now. Which leaves you. Hey, I'm not happy about it, either."

"So when you weren't eavesdropping, what didn't you overhear?"

"That you aren't going to turn Jessica in to a vampire. Good call, by the way. Which reminds me, are you ever going to do anything about the zombie in the attic?"

"Are you ever going to drop the joke? I mean, I know you guys all know I'm scared of zombies, but this is just—"

"Betsy, I'm serious. There's a zombie in the attic."

I swallowed my irritation. Cathie had had a hard life. Or death, rather. She was lonely. She was bitchy. I was the only person she could bug. Talk to, rather.

"It's not funny anymore," I said, as nicely as I could. "And it never really was. So can you please drop it now?"

"Come up to the attic and see."

Aha! The surprise party. It was on me at last, like a starving wolf in the moonlight. Fine, I'd play along.

"Okayyyyy, I'll just pop up into the attic to check on the zombie." I looked around. We were at the top of the stairs; there were closed doors on both sides of the hall. "Uh, where *is* the attic?"

"Come on." She floated off.

"Gee, I hope nobody jumps out at me or anything. Certainly not with the new Prada strappy sandals in ice blue . . ."

Cathie shook her head. "Oh, honey. If I wasn't so bored I'd never do this to you. But I am. And so I am."

She gestured to the door at the end of the south hall. I opened it and beheld a large, spiderwebby staircase. The stairs were painted white, and in serious need of a touch-up.

"Okayyyyy . . . I'm coming up the stairs . . . here I come . . . suspecting nothing . . ."

There were light switches at the top of the stairs, which was good, because even though I could see in the dark pretty well, the unrelieved gloom of the attic was a little unnerving. I couldn't even hear anybody breathing. Maybe they were all holding their breath. My live friends, that is.

Like any attic, it was filled with generations of accumulated crap. Dust covered everything: broken pictures, beat-up desks, sofas with the stuffing popping out of the cushions. It appeared to run the length of the house, which meant it was ginormous.

Out of force of habit, I put my hand up to my nose and mouth, then remembered I never sneezed—unless something threw holy water in my face, anyway.

I took a few steps forward and heard a scuttling from behind a scratched wardrobe missing a door. Ugh! Mice. Please not rats. Just little harmless field mice who had decided to stay in the mansion for the winter. I didn't mind mice at all, but rats . . .

And what was that other smell? A layer of rot above the dust. Had someone, ugh, left their lunch up here or something? Fine place for a turkey sandwich.

Cathie pointed. "He's right over there."

"Oh he is, eh?" What a crummy place for a birthday party. But I had to admit, I would never have snooped up here for presents. "Well, he'd better watch out, because here I come."

I marched a good fifteen feet and shoved the wardrobe—which was huge, much taller than I was—out of the way. "Surpri—what the . . . ?"

At first I was genuinely puzzled. It was like my brain couldn't process what it was seeing. I'd expected: banners, presents, a group of my friends and family huddled, ready to leap up and yell "Surprise."

What I got: a hunched figure, wearing rotted clothes—everything was the color of mud. Slumped shoulders; hair the same color as the clothes. And that *smell*. God, how could the others stand it? Surely even the live people could smell it.

The figure pivoted slowly to face me. My hand was back up, but this time to prevent a gag instead of a sneeze.

I could see bone sticking out of the remnants of what might have once been a white dress-shirt sleeve. Bone? That wasn't bone. It was something else, something gray and weird. It was—

"Nice zombie costume," I managed. Complete with authentic stink and rotted clothes and—this was a great touch—graveyard dirt in the wig.

"Betsy, that's what I've been trying to tell you. It's not a costume. It's a real live zombie." Cathie was circling it admiringly. "The things you see when you're dead! I thought it was a movie thing."

"Nuhhhhhhhh," it said. It reached toward me. It had long fingernails, so long they started to curve under, like claws. There was dirt under every one.

I backed up a step. It compensated by taking a step closer. I couldn't bear to look in its face—and then I did. At first I thought he—he was wearing the decayed remains of a suit— was smiling. Then I realized one of his cheeks had rotted away and I could see his teeth through his face.

I had thought I was frozen with fear. No, that was too simple a word: terror. Absolute numbing terror. It was silly, but I had a lifelong terror of dead things. Especially zombies. The way they kept coming toward you

(the way this one was coming toward me now)

and the way they reeked of the grave

(the way this one did)

and the way they moaned and reached for you and nothing stopped them, no matter what you did, they came and came

(the way this one was coming)

and I thought I was frozen with fear, thought I could never move, but somehow I was backing up. Internally, yeah, I was frozen, I couldn't make myself speak, scream, figure out where the door was, reason, think. But my legs were moving just fine. And that was good. Because if that thing touched me, I would die. Die for real. Die forever.

It

(he?)

reached still, and I was backed up against one of the dusty couches, and its hand brushed my shoulder, and then my internal freeze vanished like an ice cube on a July sidewalk and I let loose with the loudest scream I'd ever heard anybody scream. I sounded like a fire alarm.

I fell back over the couch and hit the floor, raising a cloud of dust. I was trying to back up and stand up at the same time while the zombie calmly walked around the side of the couch and kept coming. As a result, I was leaving a Betsy-wide track through the dust on the floor as I shoved myself along the floorboards.

I screamed again. This time words. But more fire alarm than words, because Cathie said, "What?"

I chewed on the phrase, actually coughed it out of my mouth: "Go get Eric!"

She rushed toward me—it seemed to take her forever to cross the fifteen feet or so between us. "Betsy, I can't!"

"Then get Tina! Get Marc! Get The Ant! I don't give a shit! *Help!*"

Suddenly, her hands shot through the zombie's chest. It kept coming.

"I can't! Nobody can see me but you! What do you want me to do?"

I'd shoved myself into the far wall and clawed my way to my feet. God, the stink! I could handle almost anything else except for the stink, the godawful, rotting, disgusting, fucking *stink*. "I don't know," I said, and never had I been so angry about being so dumb.

"Well, kill it! In the movies, the good guys shoot them in the head."

I didn't say anything, just knocked away its arm as it reached for me. Cathie finally remembered: "You don't have a gun. Okay, but you're not without skills. You're a vampire. Break his neck!"

But then I'd have to touch it. I couldn't bear to touch it. I'd go crazy if I had to touch it.

I grabbed its wrist and pushed. Hard. It went sprawling off into a broken coffee table, and smashed to the ground.

Okay, I'd touched it. And it hadn't been so bad. Okay, it had been crawly and awful—like touching a shirt full of squirming maggots—but there were worse things. Like—like—

I couldn't think of anything worse.

I looked at my hand and saw there was dirt and skin on the tips of my fingers. I started to cry and frantically wiped my hand on my jeans.

"Maybe it isn't trying to kill you," Cathie said helpfully from right beside me. "Maybe it's trying to communicate. You know, like I was. Maybe it came here because you're the Queen and you can help it. Please stop crying. Betsy, come on. It's not that bad. It's just a zombie. It can't even do anything to you."

Couldn't do anything? It was hurting me just by existing. It was—my hysterical brain groped for the word and caught it. It was an *abomination*. It was wrong for this thing to be anywhere, never mind my attic. It went against everything right and good and sane and normal.

It was getting up. It was coming toward me again. It was saying "Nuhhhhhhhhh" again. It was trying to touch me again. I cried harder. It seemed that crying like a B-movie heroine (the ones who always got saved at the last minute, but who was going to save me?) was going to be the way I dealt with this. Well, that was all right. Crying didn't hurt anybody. Crying never—

"Betsy, will you for Christ's sake do something!"

Here it came again. Here it reached again. Here it was touching me. Here it was showing me its teeth. Here it was pulling on me. Here it was making an odd noise—ah. It was trying to smack its lips, but they had rotted away. Smacking its lips the way a hungry fella smacked his lips as he contemplated Thanksgiving dinner. Or a big steak. Or—

Me.

Its hands were on my shoulders. The stench rose, almost a living thing. I raised my own hands. It pulled me close. I put my hands on either side of its head. It slobbered without saliva. I twisted. But of course it didn't die, of course it leaned in like a grotesque parody of a vampire and bit me, chewed on me, ate me while I screamed and screamed, while Cathie darted around helplessly and watched me get eaten, while—

—it fell down, its head twisted around so that, if it were alive, it would have been looking down on its own butt.

"Now that's what I'm talking about," Cathie said. "Whew! I thought you were really going to—Betsy?"

I had walked stiffly over to one of the couches. Sat down, almost impaling myself on a broken spring. Cried and cried and rubbed my hands on my jeans. They would never be clean. My fingers would always stink. They would always have dead meat and graveyard dirt on them. Always. Always.

CHAPTER 25

I sat on the couch and looked at the (dead) zombie. I never, ever wanted to get away from a place more than I wanted to get out of that attic, but I couldn't make myself get up and make the long walk to the door at the top of the stairs. The only thing I had the strength for was sitting on a filthy, broken couch that was so dusty I didn't know what color it was under all the dirt. That, and looking at the zombie I'd killed.

I suppose part of me was waiting for it to get up and come at me again. Like Jessica would get up and come at me if I'd gone through with it, if I'd ignored her wishes (as, truthfully, I'd been tempted to do) and made her a vampire. She wouldn't be Jessica anymore if I did that; she'd be a slobbering, crazy vampire. Fast forward ten years, by then maybe she'd have a little bit of control over the thirst. Then her new life would begin: being more careful about meals. Never aging, but getting old just the same. Pulling further and further away from the mortal Jessica, my friend, the older she got. Getting sly, like Eric and Alonzo.

Alonzo. He had made a vampire without a single thought to the consequences: for Sophie or for himself. He had killed her and gone on his way, and he had to pay. That was it, that was how it was: he fucked up, and he had to pay. What if it had been Jessica, dead in some alley in France how many years ago?

And how could I have gone to her room and asked her to let me do that? I deserved a zombie hiding in my attic. I deserved a hundred zombies.

"Why do you think it was here? How did it get in, and get all the way up here without anybody seeing?" Cathie was chattering nervously and looking at me the way you looked at a recent mental ward escapee. "What do you think it wanted?"

"I don't give a ripe shit," I said, and stood.

It took a long time to find the door.

CHAPTER 26

"Can I tag along?" Cathie asked, drifting beside me.

"I don't care."

"Well, I just thought I'd ask. Are you okay? You're done crying, right?"

"No promises." I could hear the phone ringing as I went downstairs. I'd heard Tina and Sinclair come back, which was too bad because it meant somewhere in this big house, Tina was sprinting to get the phone before it clicked over to the machine.

"I'm not here!" I yelled. Sinclair was standing at the foot of the stairs, looking up at me, still in his overcoat.

"It might be important," he teased, well aware of my antiphone leanings. Then he wrinkled his nose. "What is that smell?"

"It's a long damn story, and I'll tell you all about it on the way—"

"On the way where?"

"But will you just hug me right now?"

"Darling, are you all—" He almost staggered as I flung my arms around him. I tried to squash the traitorous thought

(why didn't you save me?)

and concentrate on the good things: Sinclair's arms around me, his good clean scent, the polar opposite of the zombie.

Cathie coughed. To be honest, I'd forgotten she was there. "I'll just, uh, catch up with you later." She vanished into the stairs.

Sinclair was rubbing my back. "What is it?"

"Alonzo has to be punished."

He pulled back and stared at me. "Does this have anything to do with Jessica turning you down?"

Now I was the one staring. "How did you know—okay, apparently I'm traveling through time about half as fast as the rest of you, but how did you know she'd say no?"

"Because," he replied, "she is a billionaire who works, even though she does not have to. I never imagined she would lie back and let you try to fix anything for her, much less something like this."

"Well, I don't want to do anything to her."

His perfect brow wrinkled. " 'Do' anything?"

"It's part of the long story. But if you were dying, wouldn't you—"

"She maintains she is not dying, only ill. Is it for us to argue?"

"No way. I just wish I'd figured that out a little earlier." I leaned my head against his neck. "I guess I thought maybe since she saw me get better so fast after Delk shot me—"

"*No one* should decide to be turned based on *your* experiences, my darling. You are unique."

"But maybe a vampire I turned would be like me!" God,

what was I saying? Had I learned nothing from the Unpleasant Attic Incident?

No, I didn't want to turn Jessica. But I didn't want to watch her die, either. It was too awful, like having to choose between your own manner of death: Ah, Miss Taylor, will you be choosing beheading or exsanguination today?

"No one is like you. You may check the Book of the Dead," he added, "if you require another source."

"Ugh, pass." The Book of the Dead was a tough read.

"So she did refuse you."

"Repeatedly." And a good thing, too.

He shrugged. "She has faith in modern medicine. It's not entirely misplaced."

"Yeah." I straightened his lapel, which was already perfectly straight, and felt his arm steal around my waist. I pushed him away, gently. "You need to get Tina. I've made a decision about Alonzo."

"I trust you will let me in on it?" he asked lightly, but he was giving me an odd look. "If it is not too much—"

He cut himself off. We both looked as Tina came hustling out of kitchen and almost ran through the hall, actually sliding to a stop in her stocking feet in front of the steps.

"Majesties!"

"Whoa, who died?" It was a joke, but then I remembered the company I was in, the events of the past, uh, *year*, and my life. "Oh, God. Who *did* die?"

"No one. I heard you wanted me and came as fast as I could. And Alonzo called to say he would be here in an hour."

"Not soon enough," I replied. "Let's go."

"Wait, we're meeting him?"

"Yeah. Right now. Get your coats. Come on."

"What's happening?" Tina asked.

"I was not aware you were meeting with him today," said Sinclair.

Me neither. Well, if Alonzo was open to a meeting, that was fine with me. "Listen, he killed Sophie and there has to be a consequence. Not a Nostro consequence, but still. So, he has to pay. Literally pay. And I was thinking, he's probably built quite a little holding for himself over the years. Right?"

"Right," Tina replied, and Sinclair nodded.

"Okay. So: he gives all his property and money to Sophie. And has to start over."

Sinclair blinked.

"Oh, Majesty," Tina began dolefully. "That is—we're talking millions. Possibly billions. And he would have nothing?"

"He'd have more than Sophie did. A cousin, friends to help him. A way to get back on his feet. Or maybe he never will. That's not my problem. He has to pay for what he did. And that's how it is."

Sinclair was looking at me like he'd never seen me before. Tina's eyes were practically bulging in surprise.

"I will support you, Elizabeth, if you feel this strongly about it."

And Tina said, "Your will is our will, Majesty."

And that was that.

CHAPTER 27

We pulled up to the hotel, Sinclair (reluctantly) handed his Mercedes keys to the valet, and walked into the hotel. It was one of those hotels that look like a nice big brownstone on the outside, a place where families lived. It cost, Tina had told me, twelve hundred dollars. A night. I assumed the beds were made of gold and the staff tucked you in every night with hot cocoa and kisses.

"A zombie," Tina murmured. She looked like she was having trouble processing everything that was happening at once. I hoped she enjoyed being a member of the "I'm freaking out" club. "I had no idea they even existed."

"We will take care of that—"

"Too late," I said.

"—after we take care of this. Perhaps I should tell him," Sinclair was saying as we trooped to the elevator. "Be the heavy, as it were."

"I'm not afraid to tell Alonzo that we're punishing him," I retorted. Shit, after the Unfortunate Attic Incident, I wasn't afraid of anything.

"Small bites, Majesty," Tina murmured.

The elevator came—ding! The doors slid open. Before I could let Tina in on my new "not afraid of nothin'" mind-set, Sinclair muttered the rare epithet.

Tina looked. I looked. We all looked. And after the night I'd had, I really wasn't all that surprised.

"He's pretty dead," I observed.

CHAPTER 28

Alonzo was in two pieces in the elevator. There was also a bloodless hole in the middle of his forehead. Sadly, he wasn't the first dead vampire I'd seen. I was mostly numb—no idea how I felt about Alonzo being dead, how he got that way, or what to do next. Not even taking the elevator up to the fifteenth floor (*WITH THE DEAD VAMPIRE INSIDE*) moved me. Well, moved me much.

Did I feel bad about a killer getting killed?

"Thorough job," Tina said, squatting beside Alonzo's head.

"Yep," I confirmed. So the killer had shot him to, I dunno, distract him, and then cut off his head while Alonzo was still trying to grow back his brain. Obviously, someone had known what he (or she) was dealing with. There was very little blood, which I'd expect, but the other five European vampires were scared shitless, which I didn't expect.

At least it was very late—not much staff to deal with. And we'd jumped in the elevator and taken it up before anyone in the lobby had seen.

Carolina and the others were sort of milling about in the hallway, if shifting back and forth and occasionally murmuring to each other could be called milling. I guess that was milling. What was milling? They weren't back there polishing grain, after all. They sure were taking the news like cool customers.

Wrenching my brain back to current events, I forced myself to look at Alonzo's body. The elevator door had been propped open, so unfortunately it was easy to take in.

The body was dressed up, he had his shoes and socks on. His head was about two feet away. One eye was wide with surprise; the other one was rolled up, looking at the ceiling. Well, he wasn't really looking at the ceiling. It just looked like he was looking at the ceiling. In fact, it looked like one big dead vampire in the elevator.

Alonzo had been killed in the private elevator, which was solely for the use of the guests on the suite floor. Tina had checked; the vampires were the only ones staying in the hotel suites.

Had they heard anything? If they had, they hadn't volunteered anything yet.

Anyway, the elevator had been brought back up to the fifteenth floor, where we all were, but there wasn't any police tape or anything because the vamps wanted to keep this one in-house. I had no idea how they could keep something like this from the cops (it wasn't a vampire hotel, after all) but I kept my mouth shut. Police involvement could only cause complications. Especially if Alonzo was correctly identified: hmm, a hundred-year-old dead guy who doesn't look a day over twenty-five! Now there's a stumper! Say, all you others, would you mind coming in for questioning? For about five-to-ten with time off for good behavior?

"What happened?" I asked.

There was a long silence while the Europeans looked at each other, and I was beginning to repeat my question, louder, when Carolina said, "Well, ah, Majesty, Alonzo called you and he left. And then he died."

So *that's* why they were so twitchy. Funny; I'd imagine ancient vampires didn't much care about imminent death, but I'd found the older they were, the more they thought they were entitled to live. It was amazing, when you sat down and thought about it.

"You guys, relax. I didn't do it. None of us did it." I looked at Sinclair and Tina, who I just remembered had mysteriously disappeared earlier tonight before Alonzo's death.

"None of us did it," Sinclair echoed. Right! Besides, he and Tina were always mysteriously disappearing. If Tina hadn't been gay, I would have had to keep a much closer eye on—

"The monarchy had nothing to do with this," Tina reiterated. I was glad she seemed to know all about it. "We assumed he had been killed in a dispute with one of you."

"Why would one of us kill Alonzo?" Carolina asked. "Why would I kill him?"

"To get in our good graces?" Sinclair suggested.

"Family doesn't always get along," Tina added.

"And for the same reasons humans kill," I said. "For money? To get property? For love? Hate? Jealousy? Revenge?"

Carolina was shaking her head; they were all shaking their heads. "No, no. Alonzo was—any differences we had were worked out decades ago. You were the only cause—that is to say, we had different opinions on what to do."

"Because of the situation with Dr. Trudeau," Sinclair said.

"That was her name? The brunette from your parlor?"

I looked away and counted to five before talking again. "What happened?" I asked, wondering if vampires had a CSI-type team they could send out for to, I dunno, vacuum for fingerprints or whatever.

"We had risen, of course, and were preparing to go out and get something to eat. David—" Carolina, the group's unofficial spokesvampire, nodded to a tall, quiet (but then, they were all quiet) gray-haired vampire who looked like a used car salesman in a good suit. "David was having someone come up; the rest of us were going out in a while. Alonzo was going to wait to dine, though, he wanted to leave right away. He was excited. He said you wanted him to come over. He—he was excited," she said again. "He was looking forward to seeing you again."

I turned to Tina. "For the record, not that I think you'd be so obvious and sloppy, but did you call Alonzo, pretending to be me, to lure him out away from his buddies, ambush him in the elevator on his way down, shoot him in the head, then cut his head off?"

"No, Majesty. I had to go to Best Buy and get a new DVD player for the game room."

"I can verify her story. I went with her." Sinclair sniffed down at Tina. "You are a gem in all things but one: you will insist on buying American."

"Can we focus, please? So after a while, Alonzo went skipping out the door, all happy to come to my house, and then a while later we came up with—blech—his headless body."

"Yes, there he was," used car salesman said. David! His name was David.

"And none of us did it," I clarified, "and none of you guys did it."

"If one of us had a grudge," Carolina pointed out, "we would hardly wait all this time, until we were here under your watchful eye, and kill him in a strange country in a strange hotel room. This draws your attention to us at a time when we have little interest in being noticed."

"Good point," I admitted. That "no attention" thing made sense, too. Getting noticed was a great way to get singled out and, well, just check the elevator for why it was bad to get noticed.

"We will take care of this," Sinclair told them. "We have a small team coming to tend the body. Do you wish to take him back to France?"

"Why?" Carolina asked. "He is dead. What difference does it make where his body is?"

Nice epigraph: *you're dead now, and who cares? Not even your cousin.*

"If you did not kill him," she continued, "then his properties are on the table, so to speak. Speaking for myself, I am most anxious to return and look into disbursement issues."

The three of us looked at each other. These guys didn't know that I had planned to give all Alonzo's stuff to Sophie. But now that he was dead, there was no reason to avenge the good doctor.

"You're not sad he's dead because you want his stuff?"

"His being dead solves a rather large problem for you, too, Majesty."

Larger than you think, honey. I pushed the thought of Sophie—an obvious suspect—aside for now. "Yeah, but—come on, the guy's dead. A friend of yours—family member—for decades? Perhaps a century? Don't you owe him something? Don't we all? I barely knew him and I sort of liked him, when

I wasn't thinking about—" Shooting him, I'd started to say, but probably that wasn't the best way to go. "Look, there's got to be something. I mean, I'm glad you guys aren't in a killing psycho rage because of this, but the poor guy got iced in a hotel elevator, for God's sake."

"What is it you want us to do?" Carolina asked. Her expression made it clear she could not think of a single idea that appealed to her.

It took me a moment, but then I realized what this group needed. What Alonzo needed. What *I* needed. "Okay, let's—okay, everybody bow your heads. Bow your heads! Okay. Uh, dear God, please—"

"You're praying? We can't pray," David said.

"Not to mention, I don't think Alonzo is with . . . Him," Tina added.

"Shut up, you guys. I'm sure you won't burst into flames if I do all the talking. I see heads are up. They should be bowed. Bowwwww." All the heads dropped like they were on a string, except for one. Sinclair's. He was looking at me and struggling valiantly not to laugh. I glared at him, but he wouldn't bow his head. Typical. I'd let the Big Man handle him another day.

I bowed mine and looked at my clasped fingers. "Heavenly Father, you may have noticed our friend, Alonzo, has run into a spot of misfortune. We're not sure where he is, but regardless, please bless him and look after him, forever and ever, and please let him be happy where he is and not scared or lonely. And, um, thanks again for all the help you've been giving me on the whole fasting-for-my-birthday thing. Amen."

"Okay," Tina said. "Now that the . . . the royal prayer is out of the way, perhaps we can get back to the business at hand."

"Which is what? We talked to these guys, other guys are coming to take Alonzo's body—we're not cops, we're not forensic scientists, and we're not journalists. We're—"

A phone began to ring. I glared around at them. "You guys! Shut that off. Hotel room phone, cell phone, whatever it is, kill it, just don't get me started on phones. Will you—"

After a few seconds of looking around, everyone looked straight down. The phone continued to ring.

It was coming from Alonzo's body.

CHAPTER 29

"The dead man's pants are ringing," Tina said, somewhat needlessly.

"Maybe it's a sales call," I said. "They have the worst timing."

Sinclair stepped into the elevator, fished around blank-faced in Alonzo's pants for a minute, then pulled out a small ringing cell phone.

He flipped it open and said, "Dr. Trudeau?"

Ooooh, snap! Except—

He held it out. "It's for you."

"Did you tell her that now isn't a good time? I mean, just because the phone is ringing doesn't mean—"

"Elizabeth."

"Okay, but I'm just saying. I mean, obviously this is an important call, but in general, if it's *really* important, they'll call back." I took the cell phone from Sinclair, who looked like he'd be happy to make me eat it. "Hello?"

"Hello, gorgeous," Liam drawled. "You having fun in the elevator?"

"Uh, is this the part where you taunt me and leave me clues?"

"Not hardly. I did it. Sophie wanted to, so I'm afraid I had to send her on a bit of a wild-goose chase so I could take care of things for her—"

I looked around at the others. "When you use euphemisms like 'take care of it' and stuff, are we, I just wanted to make sure, are we talking about the same thing?"

"I cut the smug bastard's head off," Liam said. "After I stuck my .38 in his forehead and pulled the trigger."

"Oh. Well, it's good that you got that out of your system." I didn't say his name out loud, though why I was trying to protect the maniac was beyond me. "So, uh, what now?"

"Now nothing, blondie. I just wanted to call you and let you know in case your barrel was swinging over to Sophie. Now listen close, 'cause there might be a test later: I did it. Sophie had nothin' to do with it. She didn't ask me to do it and she didn't know I was gonna go out and take care of it tonight. I told her you called and were looking for her—"

"That seems like a popular strategy today."

"—and she scooted right over to your place. Then I called Alonzo—"

"How'd you get the number?"

"He *gave* it to Sophie. Called *her* cell—she's listed up in Embarrass, since she's gotta be accessible —and left her the number in case she wanted to 'work things out.' Boy, if I didn't want to kill him before, I sure woulda after that."

"I, uh, gave him your number. He was supposed to call her and set up a meeting and apologize."

"Too late now," Liam said, totally unmoved.

I turned and walked a little ways away from the group. "Then you came over here and did it?"

"Yep. Then I came back to our room, told Sophie, and we lit on out of here. But I didn't want you guys wondering. It was me."

"Your friend must have flipped right out of her gourd," I said in a low voice, but who was I kidding? They were vampires. They could probably hear both ends of the conversation.

"Yep, she was pretty pissed at me. Still is. But we'll work it out."

"How does this affect your—your earlier plans?"

"Dunno." I could almost hear him shrug over the phone. "Don't much care right now. She'll turn me when she gets around to it. Right now, we gotta get in the wind."

"Maybe you don't have to—"

"You ever seen a vampire have a nightmare, Bets?" His voice was lower, too, either because he didn't want Sophie to hear or in response to mine. "It's awful. It's about the worst thing you ever saw. You have nightmares, Bets?"

"No," I said truthfully. "I don't dream anymore. I didn't think any vampires dreamed."

"Lucky," he said, and hung up.

I closed the phone and turned back to the group. "Okay! Where were we? Right, we were leaving."

"Dr. Trudeau's lover." Carolina, looking very relieved, glanced around at the others. "Of course! We should have guessed much sooner."

"What, you're happy?"

"No, just . . . reassured. Vengeance for a loved one is—"

"An understandable motive," Tina interrupted. "Like being

interested in taking over his properties."

"Right," Carolina said, completely missing the sarcasm.

"We're going," I said.

CHAPTER 30

"Wow!" Jessica said. "That is—wow! Liam! Sneaking over and icing the vampire—who'd have thought?" She answered her own question. "In retrospect, everyone. And it's *so* slick."

"Slick?"

"Well, Bets, what are you going to do?"

I opened my mouth, but Jessica rushed ahead. "Punish him? You can't do anything to him—he's human. If he was a vampire, you could do something, but he's not in your, what do you call it, jurisdiction. Turn him over to the cops? For what, killing a dead guy? Assuming you could find the body—which I bet, thanks to Sinclair's little gray men, I bet you can't—you sure don't want a forensic guy poking around in it."

"You're giving me a headache," I muttered.

"Sophie didn't do it, so you guys can't be pissed at her or punish her or anything. And someone *did* kill Alonzo, avenging Sophie. The Europeans won't expect you to do anything—they gave you a big hint when they were all uncaring about what to do with his body. In fact . . ." She shot Sinclair a sly look. "Am I right? Did you tell her?"

"I haven't had the chance, and besides, you're obviously dying to."

"I hate when you go all Sherlocky on me," I grumbled.

"They're gone! Aren't they gone?" she asked Sinclair. "I bet they beat feet out of here this very night."

"They are gone," Sinclair confirmed.

"What? Already? It's only—" I looked at my watch. It was eight-thirty the next night. Once we'd left the hotel, the evening had been a bust. Sinclair made feeble mention of tracing Sophie's cell through Alonzo's cell, but I waved that away (could it even be done? I didn't know from cell phone technology). Let it go. They were long gone from here, anywhere, and Liam probably wouldn't have been dumb enough to hang onto whatever phone he'd used to taunt me from Alonzo's pants. "How do you know?"

"I have been keeping an eye on them, of course," Sinclair replied, looking surprised at my abysmally stupid question. "They departed as soon as the sun set."

"They just took off? Without a word to anybody?"

"Of course." Sinclair was looking that cat that had eaten fifty canaries.

"But it was such a big deal when they came. And now they're just—what? Sneaking out of town? Aren't they afraid that'll make us mad?"

"They know it won't."

"It won't?"

"Look at it from their point of view, Majesty," said Tina. "They are not remotely sure of your power base. They wait almost a year before coming to pay tribute. While they are here, you show evidence of fasting, prayer, powerful allies—vampire and human—live through an attack by a vampire killer—"

"Delk wasn't trying to kill me," I protested. "He was just having a really shitty day."

"—publish your life story, maintain a cop and a doctor as blood-sheep—"

"The hell!"

"—kill a zombie sent here for obviously sinister reasons—"

I'd told them about Zombiefest in the car on the way to Alonzo's hotel. They had both been flabbergasted. Both denied ever seeing a zombie in their long, long lives. "We don't know if it was sent, or just wandered in."

"And, when presented with a moral dilemma, you arranged for the death of a contemporary."

"But I didn't!"

"From their point of view," she reminded me.

"Well, how dumb are they?" I muttered.

"Frankly," Sinclair said, smiling, "I am surprised they did not skulk out of town quite a bit earlier."

"So—you're happy? You're happy that those guys think I'm a royal murdering jerk."

"You should be very happy they think that—if you can bear it, Miss Congeniality."

I stuck a finger in his face. "I told you about that privately. It's private. Private information! *Not* for sharing with the class!"

"You should never have told Jessica then," Tina piped up, "because she told everyone that story."

"What?" Jessica cried when I looked at her. "You were in the Burnsville paper, for God's sake. It's not like it was a Pentagon secret."

I turned to Sinclair. "So do we ask Sophie and Liam to leave? Banish them?"

"They banished themselves," Sinclair said quietly. "They did not return to their home in Embarrass; no one has seen them in days. Too bad; I have questions."

"Questions like what?"

"Like how a farmer of modest means could have killed one of the oldest, most powerful vampires on the planet."

"A classic assassination," Tina pointed out. "He just walked up to him and—well. Alonzo was distracted, apparently. Perhaps Liam got close to him with a lie—I'll be your driver tonight, orders from the Queen, she's the one who had the call. Something. Anything."

"And he isn't a farmer," I said. "He lives in a small town, on a farm, but he doesn't work the land. He's retired from the Air Force, Sophie told me." I nearly groaned as I remembered *what* she had told me. "Where he used to teach small arms."

"Small arms?"

"Handguns," Tina clarified. "Hmm. In hindsight, someone should have been watching those two."

"I guess I thought Sophie would just wait around for—" *What? For me to make a move? For justice?* "Indefinitely," I finished. "I should have known none of this would sit well with Liam. And he wouldn't think killing Sophie's killer—I mean, I don't get the idea that it's going to be weighing heavy on his mind, you know?"

"Did killing Nostro weigh heavily on yours?" Sinclair asked.

I shook my head; if he was looking for answers, he had the wrong girl. "I'm so fucking thirsty right now," I admitted, "it's hard to get worked up about anything."

Jessica edged away.

"I don't think you have to worry," Tina teased. "You smell so bland and tasteless right now."

"Hey, that's right!" She brightened. "Vampire repellant."

"You've always been repellant," I told her gently.

"Oh, that reminds me. We're redoing the parlor—"

"The second one?"

"No, the first. All the foot traffic in there just reminds me how awful the wallpaper is. Anyway, once the walls were stripped the workmen found something really interesting."

"Interesting how? Interesting bad? Termites? What?"

"Come and see," she invited.

I followed her, groaning. What fresh hell was this? Couldn't I ever get a break? And why was Jess even bothering me with this stuff? She knew I was bored to death by anything having to do with the house; not to mention, if there was a real problem it would be her, not me, who would have to take care of it financially.

"Whaaat?" I whined, following her into the parlor.

"Surprise!" a dozen people yelled back. I stared; there was a big HAPPY BIRTHDAY swag on the far wall; the place was full of multicolored helium balloons, and people were throwing confetti at me. The walls, needless to say, were not stripped at all. Lying bitch.

"You'd think it would be harder to fool a vampire," my mother was saying, a colorful conical hat perched incongruously in her white hair. "But no."

"If the vampire is Betsy," Sinclair said, coming up and putting an arm around me, "it is not so difficult."

"Shut up. Jeez, you guys! I said, I said no parties." I was trying not to grin like a chimp. Aw! They'd gone to all this trouble. Balloons everywhere. Streamers. The aforementioned swag. A big table at the far end full of all kinds of pop and wine and even sandwiches. And a big cake at the end—double layer, chocolate frosting. If I knew Jessica's maniac attention to detail, the inside of the cake would be chocolate, the layers filled with chocolate buttercream. Hopefully someone had a blender nearby and could toss a piece in for me.

There was also a gallon of chocolate ice cream in a tub of ice. Now that I *could* have, once I mixed it with some milk and made it into a shake.

"Well, I can't stay," The Ant was saying, giving my mom a narrow-eyed look of (mature!) distaste. "I only came to drop the baby off." The baby had gotten hold of his birthday hat and was busily chewing on the end of it. I wondered how he'd like chocolate cake. How could I slip him some? It would blow all the circuits in his little head. And the kid would love it. Hee!

"I'll take him. Please, Mrs. Taylor? It's Betsy's special night."

"Oh, well, uh." The Ant looked flustered; BabyJon had only spent the night at home and, more and more frequently, my house. "Well, Laura, if you don't mind. He can be a handful."

"Oh, it's no trouble." She bent down and scooped him out of his car seat. "I'd love to have him overnight!" She took the hat away from him and he wailed. She whipped a bottle (where had she been keeping it? Her pocket?) into his mouth and the wail was shut off as he sucked energetically.

"Sorry I'm late," Detective Nick said, rushing into the room. I was amused to see him out of breath. "Did I miss the part where everyone yells surprise and she freaks out? I love that part."

Honey, you should have seen me last night.

"I ran from the car," he was saying apologetically to Jessica. "Sorry—got hung up at work."

"Hey, you're here. Have some cake." Jessica hugged him, and over her head Sinclair shot me a look. I knew what he was thinking: Nick hadn't been in the room when my mom had made her ill-conceived comment about vampires. So he missed it, so he was still fooled. Or he was still fooling us.

An issue for another time. The larger concern: the Ant wasn't leaving. She and Laura were burbling over BabyJon and the Ant actually took her coat off. Weird! Further proof that Laura's devilish charm worked on anybody, nobody how freakish or awful.

"Your father couldn't make it," my mom said through tight lips. "He's sorry." Wow, if I had a dollar for every time I'd heard that growing up—wait a minute. I think Sinclair *did*.

"It's fine." I meant it. It would be just too weird to have my dad there, too, along with—

Let's see, there was Nick. Jessica and Tina. Sinclair, Marc. The Ant, BabyJon. Cathie—yes, she had just floated in, and was waving to me across the room and talking to another ghost, a much older woman who kept pointing at me and gesturing urgently. No doubt a problem Cathie could handle herself, as she had suggested before.

Marjorie the librarian, scarfing up the free wine. Toni and Garrett. No Sophie and Liam, of course, but I actually looked around the room anyway. It made me sad; under "normal" circumstances, they could have—and would have—come. And obviously, no Delk.

I cheered up a little when I saw Carolina! Wait a minute, wha—yep, there she was, standing awkwardly in front of a bowl of potato chips.

I gestured and she came over to me at once, looking almost relieved. Not one for parties, this one. Or nervous about *this* party. "What are you doing here? I heard you guys were all on a plane out of town."

"Oh, well." She shrugged and looked down. "The others were in rather a hurry to get back—the business, you know, and various personal issues. But I—I wanted to see you, when you weren't under so much stress."

"Well, I'm glad you came." She smiled uncertainly and I took her hand. "Really, Carolina. I'm glad you're here."

"Oh, well," she said again, and looked away with a slightly more real smile. "Really, I couldn't stay away. It's been—it's been many years since I was at a birthday party. And never a surprise one."

"Yes, lucky me." I gave Jessica and Sinclair a sideways look. "Well, this one wasn't supposed to be. I remember saying repeatedly—"

"Oh, knock it off, bitch, you know you love it." Jessica waved my objection away. "Tell me you didn't love it when you saw all the shit on the walls and all these people here for *your* birthday."

"Yeah, well, my birthday isn't until tomorrow."

"A masterful way to throw you off guard," Sinclair put in (not that anybody was talking to him). "Which succeeded brilliantly, I might add."

"This is good practice for our wedding rehearsal," I told him, which wiped the smirk off his face. The big day was three months away, and I doubted if he knew what time it was or where to show up.

"So, thirty-one," Marc said, coming up to our little group.

Carolina laughed out loud, earning mystified looks from my

mother. I loved it—the one nice thing about ancient vampires is, they could make you feel young.

"Hey, I didn't not invite you over to my forbidden surprise party to have you insult me. God, look at all that pop. I could really use a big glass of Coke with a ton of ice."

"And I would get it for you," Sinclair said, "except that is not what you *really* want."

"Can you step out in the hall with me?" I asked seriously. "I wanted to ask you something about Liam."

"Oh." Sinclair looked surprised, then set down his wine glass, took my hand, inclined his head to the group, and said, "Excuse us."

He led me swiftly to the hall and asked, "What is it? Did he call again? Threaten you?"

"No, dumb ass. It was a ruse. A ploy, a subterfuge." I slung my arms around his neck and pulled him close. "It's my birthday and I wanted to get you alone."

"It is not technically . . . mmmm." He shut up (finally) and we kissed, made out, groped, and groaned in the hallway like a couple of teenagers sneaking out past curfew.

"Oh, Elizabeth, I do love you. I—ah!" He groaned as my teeth broke the skin on his neck, as I pulled the blood from him in a sweet winey flow, as I fell off the blood wagon with a big old crash. Sinclair was right beside me for the fall.

"I've been thinking," I murmured, licking his throat, his lower lip, the tip of his right fang. "This fast. It didn't prove anything. It didn't make me a better vampire." If anything, it made me a bitchier one. "It's not where and when you drink blood, it's—" I couldn't think of the rest of the platitude. How you drink it? Who you drink it from? If you have it in a fancy glass with a cocktail umbrella? Whatever. I was distracted. Possibly because he had bitten me, was sucking on my throat so hard he'd pulled me to my tiptoes. "Anyway," I managed, trying not to flail and gasp, "I'm going to drink again, but only from you. And you'll drink only from me. Right?"

"Mmmm," he said, his mouth busy on my throat.

"And we'll have a better life together than most, I bet."

He pulled back and looked at me. There was a spot of blood just below his lower lip in the shape of a comma. "No one, ever, could have a better life together. Not if they have you, Elizabeth."

"Well, then, aren't you the lucky fella." I laughed and kissed away the bloody comma. "Let's see if you say that three months from now."

"Er, three months?"

"Sinclair!"

"Right. Ah, the magic of three months from now. I await breathlessly."

"Very funny. We already don't breathe." I tried to wrestle out of his embrace, but he held fast. "Unf! Ergh! Sinclair: you *have* put this on your calendar, right?"

"Darling, it's been there for ages, I swear! Stop wriggling. Our magical, culturally meaningless evening looms before me like a sweet hippopotamus of joy."

I was soothed by his tone, then digested his words and redoubled my efforts to get away. "Dude! I wouldn't marry you if you begged for it."

He laughed and let me go. "But I would, you know." He looked at me with slightly narrowed eyes, that considering look I knew so well. "Beg for it."

I loved that look. I loved him. I started to step back into his embrace, but he seized me before I could, yanked me to him, and thrust his mouth into my neck with the speed of a striking snake. His teeth were so sharp I barely felt them penetrate. Well, I felt them penetrate, but not in my neck, if you know what I mean.

He had thrust his fingers into my hair and was holding me by the head, the other arm so tightly around my waist it was a good thing I didn't need to breathe. He drank from me like a man just out of the desert, squeezed me to him with desperate hunger, and I loved it, I would have let him hold me like that all day, take from me all night.

We were almost wrestling, moving in a tight little dance in the hallway, and I struggled free enough to bite him back, to feel his cool blood on my tongue like a rich dark wine, to feel it racing through my system, making me stronger, making me better, making me more.

Vampire.

"The party," I groaned.

"Fuck the party," he growled back.

"We can't stay out here making out."

"Exactly so. Let's go to bed."

I managed to wrench free—mostly because he let me—and stood back, wiped my mouth, and checked my shirt for blood stains. His tongue darted out and caught a rill of blood, and I fought the urge to leap back into his arms and bite it.

I remembered there were more than a dozen people less than ten feet away. Thank goodness for thick doors and walls! Yay, old houses! Like I said. "We'd better get back to the party."

"In a moment. I wanted to ask you. Will you tell me the entire story? The tale of you and the zombie?"

"Oh. I thought I—"

"1 me the Cliff Notes version. And we both pretended not

to notice that you nearly had a breakdown—and then there was Alonzo to deal with. But I want to hear everything."

"You'll laugh at me."

"Yes, of course."

I smiled; I couldn't help it. "Okay, but later. And with all the lights on. In our bed. And when I start to freak out all over again, tell me something that pisses me off."

"I will."

He picked up my hand—the one with my glorious engagement ring—and kissed it. "With me it's spiders."

"Really?"

He almost shuddered. Eric Sinclair, badass vampire king, afraid of Charlotte! "All those legs," he muttered.

I hugged him. "I won't tell a soul," I whispered. "But for crying out loud, we've got to get back to my party. It's the only thirty-first birthday I'm going to have, you know."

I stepped back to straighten my clothes, which didn't last long; he snatched me back into his arms so quickly I couldn't dodge, much less keep away. "Oh, the party. Never mind the party."

"Mind *me*, then," I said, and kissed him.

"I do mind you," he replied, and we got busy in the closet under the stairs, and it was only later that I thought about what he said and got pissed, but he just laughed at me.

Other titles by MaryJanice Davidson in the fabulously funny Undead series:

Undead and Unwed

'The day I died started out bad and got worse in a hurry . . .'

It's been a hell of a week for Betsy Taylor. First she loses her job. Then she's killed in a freak accident only to wake up as a vampire. On the plus side, being undead sure beats the alternative. She now has superhuman strength and an unnatural effect on the opposite sex. But what Betsy can't handle is her new liquid diet . . .

Undead and Unemployed

Nothing can make Betsy Taylor give up her shoe fetish – even dying and rising as the new Queen of the Vampires. Only being royally undead doesn't mean there aren't still credit card bills to be paid. Luckily, Betsy lands her dream job selling designer shoes at Macy's Department Store. But it seems there's been a string of vampire murders in town and they're all clamouring for Betsy to do something about it. The worst part is she'll have to enlist the help of the one vamp who makes her blood boil: the oh-so-sexy Eric Sinclair. Only the last time she ran into Sinclair she accidentally fulfilled an ancient prophesy – and ended up married to him...

Undead and Unappreciated

Most women would love to live as royalty, but Betsy Taylor has found that being vampire queen has more problems than perks, except for always being awake for Midnight Madness shoe sales. It may be easy to find blood (yuck) in the dark of night, but try finding a strawberry smoothie. And employees at her nightclub Scratch have been giving her nothing but grief since she killed their former boss. Some people . . .

Undead and Unreturnable

They say Christmas is a time for friends and family. But with a half-sister who's the devil's daughter, an evil stepmother, a fiend living in her basement, assorted spirits and killers running amok, and a spring wedding to plan with the former bane of her existence, Eric Sinclair, Betsy is not sure she'll survive the holidays.

Oh, right. She's already dead . . .